Walt Disney's
Santa's Workshop

BY Ann Braybrooks

ILLUSTRATED BY Jean Delarue

DISNEY PRESS
NEW YORK

ISBN: 0-7868-3026-3

Artwork inspired by
the Silly Symphony *Santa's Workshop*
and originally published in *Les Jouets de Noël*
by Disney Hachette.

ONE CHRISTMAS EVE A LONG TIME AGO, in a large but cozy house at the North Pole, Santa Claus was pacing through the halls and feeling worried. He wasn't worrying about his elves, though they hadn't yet returned from bringing in the reindeer and picking up the last few bags of mail for the year. And he wasn't worrying about the snow, though it had fallen all night long until it covered the entire North Pole like frosting on a cake.

No, Santa was worrying about a little girl named Emily. Emily was eight years old and lived at 2101 Lily Lane, in the town of Lollydale. That information was neatly entered in the big black book in which Santa kept the names and addresses of all the boys and girls in the world. But Santa had just noticed a blank space beside Emily's name. That meant that he had not received a letter from her last Christmas. And that meant poor Emily hadn't received any toys from Santa!

Santa didn't know why he hadn't noticed it
before—he always checked his lists at least twice.
In all the years he had been delivering toys, he had
never, ever skipped a child—not unless they were
naughty instead of nice. And he knew for a fact
that Emily had been nice her whole life. But the
important thing now was to make Emily's
Christmas twice as nice this year as ever before.
The trouble was, Santa hadn't received her letter
yet this year, either, so he didn't know what toys
she wanted.

Soon Santa spied the elves returning, with snow-
shoes strapped to their pointy red shoes. He
bounded down the stairs two at a time and opened
the door. He helped the elves carry the mail sacks
up to his office. Then he told them about Emily.

"I hope her letter is in one of these sacks," he
said. "Call me as soon as you find it. I need to
check on the sleigh and the reindeer."

First Santa went to check on the elves who were painting his sleigh. One elf was brushing bright blue paint on the outside, while three others touched up the shiny gold trim. Another elf was hard at work sweeping and cleaning the inside of the sleigh.

"Good work, everyone," Santa said. "I'd say the sleigh looks *twice* as nice as it ever did before!" He was glad of that. If little Emily happened to be peeking out her window when Santa stopped at her house, he wanted his sleigh to look lovelier and more magical than she could ever have imagined. And even if Emily didn't see it, some other child probably would—Santa knew that every Christmas Eve at least two or three children managed to stay up late enough and watch carefully enough to catch a peep of his sleigh.

Santa went outside and found more elves
working merrily, buffing the reindeer's hooves
and brushing their thick coats.

"Keep brushing, boys," he told them with a
smile. "I want those coats to be *twice* as fluffy as
they've ever been." Santa still couldn't stop think-
ing about Emily. He imagined her sitting beneath
a Christmas tree, searching through all the gifts
and not finding a single one with her name on it.
It always made him happy to think of all the children around the world waking up to find brightly
wrapped gifts under their Christmas trees. To
know that he'd missed one house made him feel
sad—but not for long. There was too much to do!

Santa watched the elves for another moment as they briskly scrubbed the reindeer's teeth with a large toothbrush.

Then he returned to his workshop. "Did you find it?" he called out as he entered his office. Half a dozen elves were there sorting the mail.

"Not yet, Santa," said one of the elves sadly.

Santa surveyed the stacks of letters on the floor. "What's this?" he cried, spying a piece of paper that had slipped beneath his desk. He bent down and grabbed the letter. "This is it! This is from Emily!"

One of the elves put a check mark beside Emily's name in Santa's big book. The other elves crowded around as Santa read Emily's letter out loud.

Dear Santa,

I cleaned my room today. Guess what? I found the letter I wrote you last year! It was stuck inside one of my favorite books. Now I know why I did not get a doll. But I had a good Christmas. Mommy gave me the cutest teddy bear. His name is Buttons. I love animals.

This year I want a rocking horse and a checkerboard. I promise to leave cookies out for you.

Love,
Emily

P.S. I have been good.

As Santa carried the doll back to his office, a loud gong echoed throughout the workshop. It signaled that midnight was approaching. Santa tucked the doll in his pocket, pulled out Emily's letter, and picked up a feather pen.

"Doll—check," he said, reading over the letter. "Rocking horse—check. Checkerboard—check!" He looked around his office, scratching his whiskers thoughtfully. "Now, what else can I bring Emily to make her Christmas doubly special?"

He spied a toy plane sitting on the desk. When he wound it up and let it fly, it did a loop-the-loop, buzzing right past his face.

Santa chuckled. "What a wonderful toy!" he exclaimed with delight. "It will be perfect for little Bobby James of Jonesville. And I've just had another wonderful idea—maybe I can find something extra for Emily in the windup room."

Santa rushed down the hall to the windup
room. As he stepped through the door, he had to
stop short to avoid stepping on a windup march-
ing band on parade. He chuckled with delight.
"Maybe Emily would like this little band," he said
to the elves who were testing the windup toys.

But at that very moment Santa spied a set of
windup animals—giraffes and sheep and snakes
and ducks and every other kind of animal there
was.

"That's it!" he cried, scooping up an empty sack.
"Emily loves animals—she said so in her letter."
He wound up the animals and watched happily as
they marched into the sack.

Once Emily's windup animals were packed, Santa carried the sack back to his office and added the special rocking horse, the checker-board, and the beautiful doll. Then it was time for Santa and the elves to start carrying all the sacks of toys out to the sleigh. Santa carefully placed the one holding Emily's toys on top of the others, smiling as he imagined Emily's happy face when she found the toys under her Christmas tree.

Everything was ready. The moon was just rising,
and gentle snowflakes were beginning to fall.
"It looks like Christmas to me," Santa said as he
climbed into the sleigh and grabbed the reins.
"Off we go!" He gave the elves a cheerful wave.
The reindeer sped across the snow and then
gracefully took off into the evening sky. "First
stop—2101 Lily Lane," Santa called to them. "It's
time to give a little girl a Christmas she'll never
forget!"

the world. Their sensitive instruments record even the slightest shifts in the large tectonic plates that make up the earth's crust. Tools such as these have greatly improved efforts to predict natural disasters. When Mt. Pinatubo in the Philippines awoke from its six-hundred-year slumber in 1991, for example, a team of scientists armed with seismometers, tiltmeters, and personal computers successfully predicted when the volcano would explode.

Clearly, the scientific community has made great strides in knowledge and in the ability to monitor and even predict some of nature's most catastrophic events. Prediction techniques have not yet been perfected, however, and control of these events eludes humanity entirely. From the moment a tropical disturbance forms over the ocean, for example, researchers can track its progress and follow every twist in its path to becoming a hurricane but they cannot predict with certainty where it will make landfall. As one researcher writes: "No one knows when or where [a catastrophic hurricane] will strike, but we do know that eventually it will blast ashore somewhere and cause massive destruction. . . . Since there is nothing anyone can do to alter that foreboding reality, the question is: Are we ready for the next great hurricane?"

The many gaps in knowledge, coupled with the inability to control these events and the certainty that they will recur, may help explain humanity's continuing fascination with natural disasters. The Natural Disasters series provides clear and careful explanations, vivid examples, and the latest information about how and why these events occur, what efforts are being made to predict them, and how to prepare for them. Annotated bibliographies provide readers with ideas for further research. Fully documented primary and secondary source quotations enliven the text. Each book in this series provides students with a wealth of information as well as launching points for further study.

Introduction

When Claire Kennedy moved into her new home in New South Wales, Australia, she knew that the chances of her house catching fire were high. A forest bordered Claire's property, but even though this gave her the opportunity of enjoying the presence of wild animals and vegetation, there was a downside. The trees and bushes surrounding her home might easily catch fire during the hot, dry summer and set her home in flames. Claire was lucky, and her home remained untouched by fire for nineteen seasons. But when the summer of 2001 arrived, her greatest fear came true—a forest fire was getting too close to her home.

Captain Daniel Ainsworth of the New South Wales Bushfire Brigade quickly headed toward Claire's property to make sure it would be secure. Claire's property was on the eastern side of the Pacific Highway, and the fire was burning on the west side of the highway. While Ainsworth's fire brigade was at the property, a burning leaf blew across the highway and ignited a fire on Claire's side of the highway. This fire started to block the way back to the highway, which was the safest spot. In spite of the risk, the fire brigade continued working to save the house.

"We were in no danger at the time," recalls Captain Ainsworth. "So we continued with property protection. We cleaned gutters and flammable fuel around Claire's house. We expected to be able to control spot fires and that . . . might save the house."[1]

But quickly and without any warning, a south wind came up and fanned flames into an area of dense bush, igniting it instantly. The winds increased their speed, and in a flash the fire grew to gigantic proportions, forcing Captain Ainsworth, his crew, and Claire to run for the safest spot.

"We couldn't get out, so we put the truck in a safe spot—the driveway—where there was no fuel underneath. We kept the engine going and the pump at the back of the truck going [because] typically the truck itself catches fire and must be put out as soon [as possible],"[2] recollects Captain Ainsworth. (Emergency research by Management Australia has reported that a car's gas tank is unlikely to explode in the period needed to stay inside the vehicle to use it as a shield against the deadly radiant heat of the fire front.)

Ainsworth, his crew, Claire, and her dog jumped into the truck's cabin and followed firefighter's training procedure: Ainsworth turned on the sprinkler system outside the cabin, which sprayed directly at the windshield; they covered themselves in fireproof woolen blankets; and they maintained radio contact with Rural Fire Service controllers back at the highway. It was pitch black with the smoke, and for the next eight minutes all they could hear were thirty-foot-high flames roaring over the truck.

From inside the cabin, they witnessed the tremendous power of wildfires. "It was like a bomb had exploded everywhere,"

A photo of the charred remains of a house shows the devastation a wildfire can cause.

Firefighters use their shovels to clear combustible material from the path of a wildfire in Arizona.

Claire recalls. "There was a cracking sound in the trees, the tops of the trees were blowing off and landing on things. Whole trees explode into a ball of fire."[3]

Luckily for all of them, another crew arrived in time to save them from the fire. Claire's house did not burn. But the heat around the house had been so intense that it melted everything made of plastic, like buckets lying on the ground and vinyl guttering. They melted beyond recognition. The tractor was fine, but the extremely intense heat had twisted the wheels. Claire Kennedy and the New South Wales Bushfire Brigade had experienced firsthand one of the most dangerous natural disasters in Australia in the last ten years.

Australians will not easily forget the 2001 Christmas season. The fire that almost consumed Claire Kennedy's home on Christmas Day was one of more than one hundred wildfires that spread out of control in New South Wales's national parks, threatening the capital, Sydney, and its 4 million inhabitants.

The wildfires reached as close as twenty-five miles from downtown Sydney, destroying or damaging about 170 homes and charring more than 1.24 million acres of parks and farmland. Material losses mounted to $36 million. Thousands of farm animals and wild animals died. Fortunately, not one human being perished in this inferno. Australians named this natural disaster the Black Christmas.

Wildland on Fire

A wildfire is a spectacular and sometimes frightening sight. On September 9, 1988, tourists watching Old Faithful were cheering as Yellowstone National Park's most popular geyser erupted. But their enthusiasm quickly turned into panic when park rangers urged them to leave while they still could. Flames from a fire in the Northfork area, rising two hundred feet and roaring like a tornado, were approaching Old Faithful pushed by winds of eighty miles per hour.

"Coals were pelting our backs and fist-sized firebrands were flying by our heads," recalls Rocky Barker, a local news reporter. "The area turned black as night and the howling wind sounded like a jet engine as we reached the road to the parking lot. The forest was engulfed in a wall of flame that tossed embers into the crowded area, swirling through the choking smoke like wind devils."[4]

The Northfork Fire was one of a series of fires that burned in Yellowstone National Park and in surrounding areas in Wyoming, Montana, and Idaho during the late summer of 1988. There were no human losses in Yellowstone during the fires, but about 36 percent of the park's land—about 720,000 acres—burned. Furthermore, the wildfires also burned approximately 280,000 acres of land outside the park area. The total cost of the fire reached $120 million. The Yellowstone wildfires of 1988 were among the largest in American history.

The terms *wildfire* and *wildland fire* refer to fires that uncontrollably burn the vegetation in natural or wild areas. Wildfires spread freely and, as they grow by burning more vegetation, they release large amounts of heat, light, and smoke. When particular types of natural areas burn, like forests or grasslands, people call the fires forest fires or grassland fires, to indicate clearly the type of wild area that is on fire. Wildfires are one of the most powerful forces of nature that are capable of causing major natural disasters.

When the Planet Burns

Wildfires burn the planet all year long. However, they happen more frequently from spring to early fall when environmental conditions favor their ignition—that is, when temperatures are higher, humidity is lower, winds blow faster, and lightning is more frequent than in the other seasons. The term *fire season* refers to the time of year when fires are more likely to occur.

Seasons occur at opposite times north and south of the equator. For example, during June, July, and August, it is summer in the Northern Hemisphere and winter in the Southern Hemisphere. For this reason, the fire season in the Northern Hemisphere runs roughly from April to October, while in the Southern Hemisphere it extends from October to March. This means that at any time of the year, there are regions on the planet where wildfires are waiting to happen.

In North America, the fire season lasts from early spring through October and peaks in July, August, and September. Forests in the higher latitudes of Alaska and Canada begin burning in April, and the fire season is at its maximum during the summer months.

African Fire Season

Geographical locations close to the equator—that is, within approximately thirty degrees north or south of it—do not have seasons as clearly marked as regions farther north or south of the equator. Close to the equator, the weather is hot or warm almost year-round, and the amount of precipitation varies. For example, low-satellite imagery acquired by the Defense Meteorological Satellite Program (DMSP) has shown that January is the peak season for African savanna

Smoke billows from treetops as a wildfire rages in Arizona. Minimal precipitation and strong winds allow such fires to spread rapidly.

burning north of the equator. Precipitation is scarce during this month, with the whole area receiving less than one inch of rain.

Dr. Donald R. Cahoon Jr., at the National Aeronautics and Space Administration's (NASA's) Langley Research Center in Hampton, Virginia, and his colleagues have analyzed the DMSP data. In one set of DMSP composite images, Cahoon describes "a wide band of fires . . . stretching across the savannas south of the Sahara desert. By April, savanna burning in both hemispheres is at minimum, and by June burning is at a peak [in southern Congo]. In October, the greatest fire activity across the southern African savannas occurs in the southeastern nations."[5]

Where Wildfires Burn

Wildfires can burn on all the continents of the planet, with the exception of Antarctica where ignition of fires is precluded mostly by scarce vegetation. Even though wildfires may occur in most natural habitats on the earth, they happen more frequently in some regions than in others.

Determining where wildfires occur around the world has not been an easy task. Global estimates of annual wildfires usually have relied on official reports provided by each country. But in many instances, these reports are incomplete. A report from the Committee on Forestry of the Food and Agriculture Organization (FAO) of the United Nations stated in 2001: "Comprehensive global statistics on wildfires required to make a reliable comparison on global occurrence . . . do not exist. In fact, millions of acres of woodlands [and all other forms of vegetation], as well as some forests, burn unreported each year."[6] This is mainly because people consider it unnecessary to report fires that do not risk human lives or property.

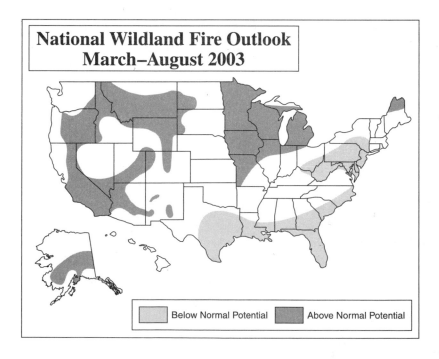

National Wildland Fire Outlook March–August 2003

Below Normal Potential   Above Normal Potential

Thanks to space technology, however, scientists studying wildfires do not need to rely on reports from individual human observers. Now, it is possible to determine the precise location and extent of fires worldwide by analyzing images of earth captured by satellites orbiting the planet.

The Fire Center of the Planet

The information provided by satellites has confirmed not only that fires occur year-round, but it has also shown that Africa is the "fire center" of our planet. This means that more vegetation burns in Africa than anywhere else on earth. After Africa, in descending order, Asia, Central and South America, Australia, North America, and Europe are the regions where most fires occur.

The reasons for large wildfires occurring more readily in Africa include the weather and the type of vegetation. The typical vegetation of the African savanna comprises a continuous layer of grass with scattered trees or shrubs that have a large proportion of thin, elongated leaves and branches that dry quickly under the sun. This type of vegetation covers approximately 6.2 million square miles of tropical Africa. Along with frequent lightning, this area has low rainfall and extremely hot weather that combine to dry the vegetation and make it highly susceptible to fire.

Fire in Tropical Forests

The tropical forests in the Amazon Basin and Indonesia have been less prone to fire than other susceptible areas because of frequent rainfall and high humidity in the region, which work against fire ignition. But starting in the 1990s, significant climate changes have occurred and they have increased the probability of fires in tropical forests. One of the most important climate-related phenomena is the weather pattern called El Niño, which is the periodic warming of the Pacific Ocean off the western coast of South America.

By the second half of the 1990s, El Niño had contributed to severe droughts worldwide, which turned moist rain forests

Striking Facts About Lightning

Around the year 2000, Dr. Hugh Christian and Dr. Richard Blakeslee and their NASA colleagues at the National Space Science and Technology Center in Huntsville, Alabama, used new detector systems orbiting Earth in satellites to monitor lightning. They discovered for the first time that the global distribution of lightning depends on the latitude, longitude, and time of the year.

This new technology has provided a more accurate picture of lightning activity. The scientists discovered that lightning occurs half as often as previously estimated. Before their studies, people thought that about one hundred lightning flashes per second struck the planet. But Christian and his colleagues discovered that lightning peaks in the Northern Hemisphere in summer at forty-five flashes per second.

The scientists also discovered that the place where people have the best chance of getting hit by lightning twice is central Africa because there are thunderstorms year-round as a result of weather patterns, air flow from the Atlantic Ocean, and enhancement by mountainous terrain. Lightning is also more active in the hemisphere that is experiencing summer.

The data analyzed by the NASA team has also shown that lightning strikes land more often than water. From December 1997 through January 1998, 90 percent of lightning was over land. During summer in the United States, lightning strikes Florida more than any other state, with Colorado, New Mexico, and Arizona also receiving a heavy share.

into drier habitats with an increased chance to burn. Consequently, during 1997 and 1998 the number, frequency, size, and duration of rain forest wildfires increased to levels never recorded before. Millions of acres burned in large areas of the Amazon Basin, Central America, Mexico, and Southeast Asia. Even areas that had not burned in the last one hundred years, like the Amazon rain forest in Brazil and the cloud forest of Chiapas, Mexico, were severely damaged by wildfires.

Worldwide, the wildfires in 1999–2000 were less serious than the fires of 1997–1998. Nevertheless, Indonesia suffered widespread wildfires in 1999 and 2000, although on a smaller scale than in 1997 and 1998. In the year 2000, the major wildfires in the world took place in Ethiopia, the eastern Mediterranean area, and the western United States.

Smoke and flames engulf the Amazon rain forest in 1998. Drought caused by El Niño made the rain forest susceptible to wildfires.

Fires in the United States and Canada

In the United States and Canada, forests are the principal feature of the landscape, covering one-half of Canada's territory and one-third of U.S. land. In the United States, normally most fires take place in the northwest and west and (in descending order) in the south, east, and northeast regions.

How susceptible North American forests are to fire depends largely on how much precipitation they receive during the winter, spring, and summer months. If these lands suffer severe drought during the months preceding the fire season, the forests will be dry and therefore highly susceptible to wildfires. The severity of the U.S. fire season depends largely on the temperature of the Pacific Ocean off South America. When La Niña, a periodic cooling of those waters, predominates, the Northwest has wet weather and the southern states suffer dry weather during the months preceding the fire season.

Before the 2000 fire season began, hot and dry conditions prevailed in most of the United States. These were attributed to a weakening of La Niña weather pattern and a corresponding strengthening of El Niño. According to a report on the highlights of the 2000 fire season by the National Interagency Fire Center (NIFC): "All the wrong conditions were in place last summer: hot, dry weather, wind, low relative humidity, a source of ignition in the form of dry thunderstorms that rattled across the West; and absence of the seasonal monsoons in the Southwest."[7] In 2000, the combination of "all the wrong conditions" produced the worst fire season in the United States in the last half of the twentieth century.

Measuring the Severity of Wildfires

Experts describe the severity of the fire season in terms of the number of fires and the number of acres of land and tons of vegetation burned. The acreage and tonnage statistics usually provide an accurate description of the extent of the fires and damage caused by them. The higher those values, the worse the fire season.

Fire Severity in the United States

In the United States from 1991 to 2000, an average of 106,400 wildfires burned each year, most of them during the fire season. During that period, some years were worse than others. More wildfires burned in 1995 than in any other year, a total of 130,019 fires. In 1998, there were 81,043 fires, the lowest number for the decade.

The annual average number of acres burned in the United States from 1991 to 2000 was 4,083,347. In the year 2000, a record high of 8,422,237 acres of land burned. Usually the fire season works northward each year, growing less intense in the south. "Not so in 2000," according to the NIFC in Boise, Idaho, the federal agency that coordinates all wildfire activities. "By midsummer, nine of the eleven Geographic

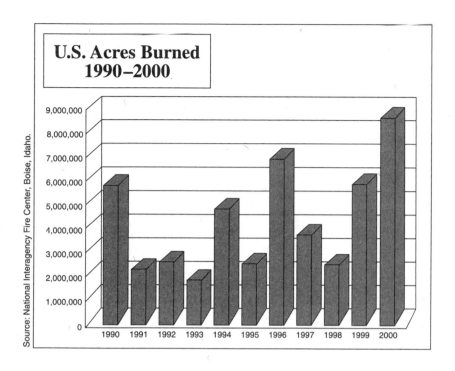

U.S. Acres Burned 1990–2000

Source: National Interagency Fire Center, Boise, Idaho.

Areas of the country had fires burning in them. Only Alaska and New England states were spared."[8]

Then came the 2002 fire season, the second most severe nationally since 1991 and the worst in many years for some western states. "This season will be remembered for its large timber fires. Colorado, Arizona, and Oregon recorded their largest fires in the last century,"[9] reported the NIFC on October 11, 2002. In contrast, the year 1991 recorded the lowest number of acres burned, a total of 2,237,714 nationwide.

Each year a large amount of live and dead vegetation, called biomass, is burned worldwide. Darold Ward, a researcher at the U.S. Department of Agriculture (USDA) Forest Service, has worked on the biomass studies and obtained impressive results. "An estimate of 6 petagrams—about 6.3 billion tons—of biomass is burned each year. About 80 percent of all biomass burning takes place in tropical countries. About 3 to 5 percent of the total is burned here in the United States."[10]

What Causes Wildfires

A wildfire starts when a source of heat makes contact with flammable natural fuel. Dead tree trunks, an accumulation of dry bushes or withering grasses, and live trees or shrubs are examples of natural fuels. The most common source of natural heat capable of igniting fires is lightning, which usually kindles more than 80 percent of the fires in remote, uninhabited wildland, like the Russian boreal forests.

Other natural sources of heat are capable of igniting fires, but this occurs much less commonly. For example, during the eruption of Mount Etna in Italy in October 2002, lava burned trees as it slid down the mountain and burning ashes and debris launched from the boiling crater traveled long distances and started fires in areas miles away from the volcano.

Half the world away from Italy, in Australia, there are catastrophic wildfires called bushfires, and during adverse weather conditions, firefighters can do nothing to stop them. "Southeastern Australia has the greatest wildfire hazard in the world," explains a spokesman for Emergency Management Australia. "Really large bushfires burn until stopped naturally by rain or lack of fuel."[11] In Australia, as elsewhere, lightning and human activities cause most wildfires.

How Lightning Causes Fires

Lightning is a concentrated source of energy. It may have a temperature as high as three thousand degrees Fahrenheit, which is high enough to ignite almost any fuel. In "The Secrets of Fire," author Susan J. Tweit gives specifics: "Up to a trillion watts of energy zap the contact point in multiple strokes."[12]

Lightning is a discharge of electricity in the form of a giant spark that moves between clouds, within a cloud, or between clouds and the ground. Cloud-to-ground strikes make up about 25 percent of total lightning activity.

As it travels along its path, lightning heats the air around it to a temperature of about fifty thousand degrees Fahrenheit—hotter than the surface of the sun. This sudden increase in temperature causes a rapid expansion of the air in the region through which the lightning passes, the lightning channel, creating a shock wave that we hear as thunder. Lightning has a higher chance of starting a wildfire when it occurs in the absence of rain—experts call this "dry lightning."

How People Cause Fires

When performed carelessly, human activities are also capable of igniting wildfires. Indeed, in most seasons humans tend to cause the majority of the fires. Reports from the NIFC indicate that in the United States human activities directly and indirectly

---

What Is in a Wildfire's Name?

Every wildfire has a name, and these days their names usually come from a distinctive geographic feature identified by the first firefighter on the scene. But this was not always the case. The stories behind these names appear in "Wildfire Names Always Tell a Story," which comes from www.azcentral.com.

- In 1984, firefighter Jan Rice was carrying a box of cheddar cheese crackers and named the fire he was fighting in Colorado, the Cheddar Cheese Fire.
- U.S. Forest Service employee Larry Klock named a 120,000-acre blaze running over the pine-covered foothills of the Pike National Forest of Denver the Hayman Fire after a ghost town in the area.
- Colorado's Storm King Fire is named after the mountain where it killed fourteen firefighters in 1994. The official name of this fire is the South Canyon Fire, and it is one of the worst wildfire disasters in U.S. history.
- In 2002, Colorado's Coal Seam Fire got its name after a long-smoldering underground coal fire that burst to the surface igniting brush and trees. This fire burned more than 120,000 acres and destroyed twenty-nine homes near Glenwood Springs.
- The favorite fire name of Dave Nyquist, chief of the Lefthand Canyon Fire Department, is Devil's Bathtub. "The fire was around a big rocky knob that looked just like a bathtub, and there was water inside, but it was a lot hotter than you'd want to get into," he said.

associated with wildfire ignition include campfires, smoking, malfunctioning equipment, and sparks from trains.

Wildfires caused by human activities can be as large and dangerous as fires ignited by lightning or other natural causes. "A woodcutter, gathering wood in the tinder-dry Targhee National Forest within 200 yards of the Yellowstone border, dropped a cigarette. He left."[13] The Targhee Fire was one of the fastest growing of the fires that contributed to the Yellowstone catastrophe of 1988.

Incendiary fires, those caused purposely by unscrupulous people, can also result in major natural disasters. Some of these not only destroy large natural areas but also threaten people's lives and totally or partially ruin property. Human hands started some of the major fires that savaged large territories in Oregon and Colorado during 2002, resulting in significant property losses and costing billions of dollars to public and private institutions. People who cause incendiary fires can be prosecuted by the law, sentenced to imprisonment, and fined thousands of dollars.

According to the NIFC, during the 1988–1997 period, humans caused 88 percent of the fires, and lightning ignited the remaining 12 percent. But lightning-ignited fires were larger and consumed 52 percent of the land burned, while human-caused ignitions burned the rest.

Outside the United States, human activities not only cause the majority of the fires but those fires also burn most of the land year after year. In areas of Africa, Mexico, and Central and South America, it is a very old tradition to start wildfires with the purpose of clearing land for agriculture, hunting, or other life-sustaining activities. In large territories in central and southern Africa, for example, where savannas predominate, people deliberately start almost all the wildfires that burn the land every year.

Global Consequences of Fires

Most wildfires are rated small. Some experts consider a wildfire small when it has burned a natural area smaller than three

Positive and Negative Lightning

During a thunderstorm, clouds form at tens of thousands of feet into the atmosphere, where temperatures are as low as thirty-two degrees Fahrenheit—water's freezing point. Under these conditions, precipitation forms as ice crystals, hail, and rain. Driven by winds, ice particles of different sizes collide and become electrically charged, some with a positive charge, and others with a negative charge. The wind carries the positively charged ice crystals to the top of the clouds, while the heavier negatively charged hail collects at the bottom of the storm clouds. This process creates a positive electrical charge at the top of the clouds, while the bottom of the clouds develops a negative charge.

In negative-lightning strikes, invisible, negatively charged streamers surge toward the ground from an extremely charged cloud base. As they approach the earth, invisible, positively charged streamers are attracted upward from trees and other objects on the ground. When the positive and negative charges make a connection, a surge of electrical current moves from the ground to the cloud in a visible "return stroke" called lightning.

This entire sequence of events takes only a few seconds. People standing under a thunderstorm who feel their hair rising are in grave danger: Positive charges are rising toward the clouds in the immediate area, signaling that lightning may be about to strike.

Flashes of lightning illuminate the nighttime sky during a thunderstorm.

The development of positive-lightning flashes is similar to the negative strikes, except that positive strikes usually originate in the positive zone of the clouds and surge toward the ground. Almost instantly, streamers of negative charges rush from the ground to intercept the positively charged streamers, and when they make a connection, positive lightning occurs.

Smoke clouds the sky above the remains of a forest consumed by wildfire. Large fires have long-term effects on people, animals, and the environment.

acres. Small fires usually do not cause major damage and are relatively easy to control. About 75 percent of the world's wildfires are considered small fires, and they go unnoticed by the majority of the public.

However, even though only 25 percent of the fires around the world are rated large—because they burn areas larger than three acres—large fires are responsible for 80 percent or more of the total biomass burned. Large fires savage wildland and property, they affect people's health, and their consequences extend beyond the area burned, affecting the health and daily activities of people on a global scale.

During 1997 and 1998, large fires had dramatic consequences for most of the planet. In Indonesia alone, these fires consumed about 22 million acres of land and forest area. The smoke produced by the burning of these tropical forests spread over a large segment of the Asia-Pacific region and caused a high number of health problems and some deaths. Furthermore, the dense cloud of smoke markedly reduced visibility to the point of interfering with transportation systems, which substantially disrupted a multimillion-dollar tourist industry. All this added considerably to the economic and social cost of the fires, which experts estimate to be on the order of $6 billion.

Fire Frequency Is Increasing Worldwide

The United Nations Environmental Program considers the 1997–1998 fires "the most damaging in recorded history."[14] The fires were so damaging because nearly all types of forests and other types of vegetation burned. Fires consumed forests growing in the arid and semiarid zones of the world, as they do every year. But some tropical forests also burned, including large habitats in the Amazon area that had not burned in recent memory.

Changes in weather patterns are not the only reason for increased wildfire activity worldwide. As the human population grows and moves into wildland areas, significant portions of these areas have been lost to fire-related activities, from accidents caused by unattended campfires to deliberate burning of forests to transform them into fields for farming. Fire-related activities are the primary cause of deforestation.

On the other hand, scientists have realized that not all the consequences of wildfires are negative for the environment. Wildfires are a natural and important component of the planet's habitats, with the power to rejuvenate the environment and allow the circle of life to continue. To attempt to suppress all fires would cause more damage than benefits in the long term.

Wildfires have burned the earth for 400 million years, and they will continue to do so in the future. The greatest challenge for present and future generations is not to address the impossible task of stopping all fires but to learn to live with these often unpredictable phenomena while protecting people and property.

How Wildfires Happen

The nature of fire has puzzled the human mind since ancient times. What is fire? Which forces mold its unpredictable behavior? These questions presented a major challenge because fire is an extremely complex natural phenomenon. Ancient humans thought fire had a mind of its own and treated it as a living entity.

By the early eighteenth century, philosophers had concluded that fire was a substance. In 1772, however, Antoine Lavoisier, the father of modern chemistry, showed with simple experiments that fire is not a substance but the product of a chemical reaction that requires oxygen and releases heat and light. The French chemist and others went on to prove that fire has definite physical and chemical properties, and these characteristics are the same whether it is a flame burning a birthday candle or one-hundred-foot-high flames consuming a forest.

The Fire Triangle

Fire is the result of a chemical process called combustion, from the Latin word *combustus*, which means "to burn up." Combustion is a rapid form of the chemical reaction called oxidation. During combustion, heat causes substances to combine with oxygen in the air to produce heat, light, and gases, like carbon dioxide and water vapor, as well as solids, like char, tar, and ashes.

As Lavoisier observed, combustion takes place only if three elements—heat, fuel, and oxygen—are present simultaneously in sufficient amounts. This relationship among the three elements is represented as a "fire triangle." Removing just one of the elements will extinguish a fire. Thus, people may put out a campfire by pouring water on it. This removes heat, causing the wood sticks or coals to cool below the level at which they are hot enough to keep on burning. A campfire also can be extinguished by covering it with dirt, that is, by preventing the oxygen in the air from feeding the fire. Combustion also will stop if fuel is removed, as when wood logs or coals are cleared away from a campfire.

Heat

Heat is the force or source of energy that starts all wildfires. A fire may start slow, creeping along with little oxygen under a cover of vegetation, or fast, as when lightning strikes a tree making it explode into a ball of flames. To grow and propagate, however, a fire must produce enough heat to sustain itself. There are three methods of heat transfer that keep fires burning: conduction, convection, and radiation.

Most natural fuels, like wood, are poor conductors of heat, so the type of heat transfer that occurs the instant a person

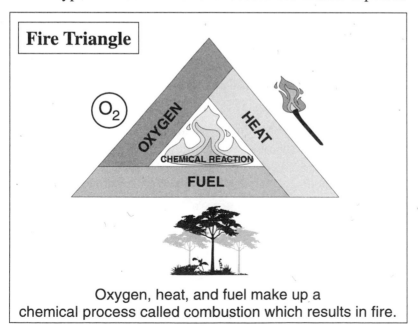

Fire Triangle

O₂   OXYGEN   HEAT   CHEMICAL REACTION   FUEL

Oxygen, heat, and fuel make up a chemical process called combustion which results in fire.

Fires Start Slow and Fast

Different scenarios may arise after a summer thunderstorm blasts the ground with lightning, and one of the most important factors that determine the consequences of a lightning strike is the location of the strike.

In one case, for example, dry lightning strikes a dead and withering snag lying on the ground and produces a thin, waving column of smoke that ascends above the dead tree trunk. Suddenly, minuscule flames appear and start crawling under the ground cover, burning a path through a thick layer of organic debris topped with dead twigs, leaves, branches, pinecones, and other plant and animal remains. The fire continues smoldering—burning without large flames—for many months, never visible above the ground. When cooler weather approaches, rain or snow extinguishes the fire after it has burned about two acres. These fires usually go unnoticed.

When summer lightning zaps a live tree, however, its sap superheats immediately. The sap expands violently and the tree trunk explodes, shooting foot-long lumps of burning wood tens of feet away. As the burning wood lands on tall accumulations of dry grass, the grass ignites quickly and the flames, fanned by gusts of wind from the storm, move to a surrounding group of small trees, climb to the crowns of larger trees, and uncontrollably consume twenty thousand acres or more of forest.

touches the hot surface of an iron—conduction—is of little importance in the initiation of wildfires.

Convection, on the other hand, often encourages the development of wildfires. During this heat-transfer process, the air itself carries heat to new fuels. For example, as bushes burn in a forest fire they produce heat that warms up the air around them. As the hot air rises, it heats up the vegetation above the ground.

If heat transferred to fuels by radiation, it would travel as rays coming out of a heat source. A familiar example is when burning logs in a fireplace radiate heat to a person nearby. Radiation is also an important means of heating up fuel during wildfires. When a line of flames from a fire front radiates heat in all directions, it heats up the fuels ahead and increases their chances of bursting into flames.

Fuel

Although gasoline and other fuels used for motor vehicles are indeed highly flammable, technically speaking, fuel for a fire is any material that can combust. In nature, fuels are a mixture of dead and live vegetation on top of, under, or above the ground. Natural fuels—wood, plant stems, branches, grass, and leaves—comprise mostly cellulose, lignin, extractives, minerals, and water.

The complex carbohydrate cellulose, one of the most abundant materials on the earth's surface, is a major component of all plants. Cellulose is an excellent building material, and plants use it to construct all plant structures.

Cellulose will resist burning until it reaches about 480 degrees Fahrenheit, but at a temperature of 620 degrees Fahrenheit, it will suddenly break down and release large quantities of flammable gases, which will burst into flames releasing large amounts of heat.

Lignin, an essential component of all plant life, does not burn as well as cellulose. At temperatures close to 842 degrees Fahrenheit, however, it releases certain flammable products.

Cellulose Molecule

The structure of a cellulose molecule forms strong fibers and is a major component of all plants. It is a source of fuel for wildfires and produces large volumes of flammable gases once the molecule is broken down.

Extractives, which are chemicals such as ethers, waxes, terpenes, and oils present in leaves and needles, release large amounts of flammable gases. Extractives allow living fuels to combust despite their large water content. This assistance is possible because when the flammable gases burn at temperatures below 212 degrees Fahrenheit, the heat produced accelerates the evaporation of water in plants and makes it easier for the fuel to burst into flames.

Some plants and trees have particular chemicals that make them more flammable than others. The eucalyptus trees that abound in Australian forests contain extractives called resins that are highly flammable. Resins melt and drip on fresh fuels, setting them on fire; sometimes heated-up resins may explode.

Combustion Resistance in Natural Fuels

Natural fuels contain minerals that can modify the chemical processes that occur during combustion, with the result that fewer flammable gases are produced and less heat is released. The discovery of minerals that inhibit combustion led scientists to design fire retardants to control fires.

Water, the most variable of the components of natural fuels, is the principal determinant of the course of their combustion. For live fuels, water represents between 80 and 200 percent of their dry weight, while for dead fuels the proportion is between 1 and 30 percent of the dry weight.

The water content of live fuels varies with the type of fuel, seasonal growth patterns, and drought. For dead fuels, moisture content depends on precipitation and atmospheric relative humidity.

Moisture slows down the combustion by cooling the reaction zone and interfering with oxygenation. Before a piece of wood can heat up enough to burn, it must lose its water. As heat builds up, the water in different parts of the wood reaches the boiling point and turns into water vapor. Only when all the water has been evaporated can the temperature of the wood continue to increase and reach combustion levels.

Another Way to Look at Wildfires

Fire behavior is so complex that sometimes it might help visualizing it in a different way. Some fire experts describe wildfires according to the location of the fuels. These types are ground fires, surface fires, and the spectacular crown fires of the type that swept through Yellowstone Park in 1988, advancing along three-hundred-year-old trees and burning tens of thousands of acres.

In ground fires, the fuel is the layer of organic material that accumulates directly under the ground level, beneath the surface covered with leaves, needles, and twigs. Ground fires do not produce flames, they smolder or burn like glowing embers. Ground fires occur, for example, after the firefighters have extinguished the flames burning a group of bushes. Even though the flames are no longer a threat, there are usually layers of organic matter smoldering under the ground beneath the bushes that may produce flames if a gust of air revives the flames. The firefighters' job is to remove the smoldering material to make the fire safe.

A firefighter douses the smoldering embers of a ground fire.

On the other hand, surface fires burn grasses, bushes, and other plants, as well as leaves, branches, fallen trees, logs, and small trees, as the flames creep along the surface of the ground. Many of the fires that burned around Sydney, Australia, in the 2001 Black Christmas season were surface fires that fiercely consumed large amounts of bushes and shrubs.

The most dangerous fires, crown fires, burn the canopy of trees that are higher than four to six feet above the ground. Crown fires move from treetop to treetop and are fanned by strong winds and fed by dry fuels.

Fuel Physics

For a fire to burn, heated fuels must mix with air containing at least 16 percent oxygen. The earth's atmosphere is 21 percent oxygen, so this is not a limiting factor for most wildfires. When oxygen combines with flammable substances in the fuels by the process of oxidation, the reactions yield new substances and also release heat. The fire is then able to sustain itself by triggering more oxidation.

How fuels burn depends not only on the amount of oxygen available but also on such physical characteristics as the fuel's thermal conductivity and whether it is "thick" or "thin."

In the context of wildfires, thermal conductivity is the property of a fuel that allows it to transfer heat from its surface to its interior. Since natural fuels are typically poor conductors of heat, scientists often use another physical property to describe how fuels burn. This is the surface-to-volume ratio, which indicates the susceptibility of fuels to heat; it is calculated by dividing the surface area of the fuel by its volume. In practical terms, the result gives an idea of how "thick" or "thin" fuels are—the higher the ratio, the thinner the fuel.

In general, if two pieces of fuel made of the same material receive the same amount of heat, the thinner fuel will burn quicker than the thicker fuel. Thin, fine fuels like blades of grass usually burn quicker than thicker fuels, like a wood log, with their smaller surface-to-volume ratio.

Fine fuels burn quickly because their surface warms up rapidly by the heat-transfer processes of convection and radiation; the interior, which undergoes the much slower process of conduction, heats up rapidly too because the fuel is thin. Thicker fuels—like wood logs—take longer to combust: The surface will warm up quickly, but the thick interior will take much longer to get hot by conduction.

The Life Cycle of a Wildfire

A wildfire proceeds from preignition to ignition to combustion, and finally to extinction. Preignition is achieved by means of dehydration and pyrolysis. During dehydration, heat evaporates any moisture in the fuel that has been inhibiting combustion; in pyrolysis, heat induces the chemical reactions that yield the materials required for actual burning.

Before a forest or savanna can burst into flames—the moment of ignition—the dehydrated fuel must be generating enough heated gases and solids to support combustion. When pyrolysis produces gases, flaming combustion will be the result. A fire in a fireplace is a familiar example of this phenomenon: The flames are from the burning of the gases given off by the logs, not from the logs themselves. When the products

Flames lick at the inside of a hollow tree. Chemical reactions inside the dry tree trunk create gases, resulting in the flaming combustion seen here.

of pyrolysis are solids, there will be glowing combustion, as represented by live embers.

Wildfires typically show two areas of combustion: the flaming front and the glowing area. The flaming front, or fire front, is the zone of a fire where the common form of combustion is flame. Behind this zone, fuels will mostly burn by glowing combustion.

Wildfires are not stationary; their flaming front moves. To describe a moving fire, experts report the rate of spread and the fire-line intensity. The rate of spread provides information about how fast the flaming front is moving as a whole into new fuels. The fire-front intensity indicates how much energy

Glowing combustion behind the flaming front of forest fires threatens firefighters because it produces large amounts of smoke.

or heat the flaming front is releasing as it moves.

Where fine fuels predominate, flaming combustion will consume most of them in a matter of minutes. But when thick or large fuels are the majority of the fuel available, they may burn for days, even weeks, by glowing combustion and slowly release smoke and heat. Although much less impressive than flaming combustion, glowing combustion might be a problem for fire managers. When the zone of glowing combustion is large, it may provide a persistent source of ignition and produce large amounts of smoke that may become a serious health problem.

Eventually all fires will go out, mainly because there are no more fuels to burn. Extinction also takes place when the amount of one of the other two elements of the fire triangle—oxygen or heat—drops below a critical level. As opposed to ignition, which is instantaneous, extinction is a gradual process in which the heat slowly diminishes until it is all lost and the fire dies out.

Wildfire Growth

The manner in which a wildfire grows and spreads is difficult to predict because it depends on various factors: the weather, winds, and variations in soil moisture, fuels, and terrain. In spite of the complexity of fire behavior, a fire generally spreads in a predictable sequence of events.

At the beginning, the flames burn only at the "point of ignition," and then they move outward as they burn the vegetation immediately around it. As the flames move forward, pushed by winds toward new fuels, the perimeter defined by the flames tends to grow into an elliptical shape. The terrain itself may also help shape a fire like an ellipse. If the fire is burning toward fuels on the slope of a hill, the vegetation on the inclined area is closer to the fire than the fuels on the flat terrain around the hill. The fire will grow faster uphill, consuming the fuels on the slope. As the fire progresses, many factors will alter its shape, including changes in the direction or speed of winds and the presence of natural obstacles, such as boulders, bodies of water, slopes, and ridges.

When describing a wildfire, experts use the term "head" to refer to the end of the fire that the wind blows toward new fuels. The head of the fire progresses faster than its sides, or flanks. On the other hand, the rear of the fire is slanted in the direction of the already burned fuels, and with less fuel available, these flames move outward more slowly. Fires that advance against the wind or down slope are called "backing fires."

As a wildfire grows, its shape will change from an elliptical to an irregular form characterized by "fingers," "pockets," and "islands." Fingers are small extensions of the perimeter that extend out from the main body of the fire, while pockets are unburned zones between fingers and the main fire. Pockets that are completely isolated within the burning main area are called islands.

A wildfire will grow as long as it steadily produces an amount of heat within the range of ten to thirty British thermal units per minute. Under these circumstances, the environmental conditions will primarily dictate wildfire behavior and spread. Heat transfer to new fuels will take place by radiation mostly, or by radiation and convection.

Growing Out of Control

If either the fire intensity or the rate of spread increases significantly, then a steadily growing fire will make the transition to the category of large fires. The transition may occur when the fire encounters extremely dried fuels, fuels with extractives that release very high amounts of heat, or fast winds. It might take only about fifteen minutes for a fire to grow into a large blaze.

As the heat output increases, the flames become larger and the possibility of controlling the wildfire decreases. Fire-front intensity is expressed in British thermal units per second per foot. A blaze with a fire-front intensity of 100 British thermal units per second per foot and with flames about 3.8 feet high is considered to be out of control by manual methods. When fire-front intensity reaches or exceeds 500 British thermal units per second per foot and the flames are above 7.8 feet high, the chances of controlling the fire by any human intervention are null. Such fires can be controlled only by extensive changes in the weather, like the development of abundant precipitation or a significant temperature reduction. A change in the abundance or type of fuels available also affects the chances of controlling the fire. When the large fire has returned to less intense conditions, then human intervention has a chance to control it. Large fires exist in two categories: conflagrations and mass fires.

Conflagrations—also called runaway fires—typically show a large rate of spread. They happen when wind-driven oxygen mixes with mostly low-lying fuels, like abundant dry grasses, and convection transfers most of the heat in the growing wildfire. These factors cause the fire to spread rapidly, consuming a large area fast, but producing a low amount of heat.

Mass fires, or firestorms, characteristically release very large amounts of heat. In this case, wind-driven gases enter the fire, fuels are mostly vertical like in a forest, and heat transfer occurs mainly by radiation. The extremely powerful winds create strong indrafts, which prevent the fire from moving forward by confining its supply of oxygen and its transfer of heat to the actively burning area.

Large fires spread and grow by mechanisms that are different from those that control smaller fires. In their book *Fire in the Forestry*, Craig Chandler, director of Forest Fire and Atmospheric Sciences Research, and his colleagues wrote that "large fires 'make their own weather' because they can noticeably alter the temperature, humidity, and wind fields in their vicinity over what would be expected at that time and location without a fire nearby."[15]

How Large Fires Spread

Large fires typically spread by a combination of the following processes: crown fires, spotting, convective columns, and fire whirls. "Crown fires" move on by burning the crowns of trees, potentially becoming very large, intense, and destructive, like the crown fires that occurred at Yellowstone in 1988. When asked how to control a crown fire, one ranger had a simple response: "Get out of the way and pray . . . for rain."[16]

One of the reasons crown fires and other kinds of large fires become so large is because they often throw embers far ahead of the main fire. This is called "spotting." A fire is spotting

The flames of this Colorado crown fire extend high above the treetops. Crown fires are particularly difficult to control because they spread so quickly.

when the hot air rising from the flames transports embers or firebrands, which are pieces of burning wood, upward and over to fuels ahead of the fire, where they start new fires. "In Tasmania in 1983, one ember spotted 47 miles from the source," recalls Tony Mount, a fire research specialist. "Curled strips of eucalyptus bark that were burning inside were transformed into flaming javelins by 100-miles-per-hour winds."[17]

A "convective column" is a large, dense plume of smoke that rises from a fire pushed by heated air in motion, or convection. The larger the column, the more cool air around the fire gets pulled into the fire. This creates an indraft that turns

An immense convective column rises from a forest fire. These columns of smoke pull cool air into the fire that feeds the flames.

the blaze into a whirling tower of fire. During the 1988 Yellowstone fires, when Douglas Brown was flying a helicopter over the area he saw "300-foot flames and huge convection columns down the canyons"[18] that created indraft winds that for some time prevented him from leaving the area for safety at the helibase.

In his book *Fire*, expert John Lyons describes a "fire whirl" like the one that destroyed the town of Peshtigo, Wisconsin, in 1871. "It begins when a fire sends up a convection plume of hot gases that draws a flow of air . . . inward at the bottom with sufficient force to dominate other local air circulation. . . . [Then] the in-pouring wind begins to develop a rotation, usually counterclockwise in the Northern Hemisphere." The result is a fire-induced cyclone, which "is similar in all other respects to the more common cyclones, tornadoes, and typhoons and it generates the same enormous forces,"[19] explains Lyons.

The Peshtigo Fire affected Wisconsin and Michigan on October 8, 1871, burning 1.2 million acres in Wisconsin and 2.5 million in Michigan. The fire killed more than two thousand people as hurricane-force winds turned the large fires into a massive firestorm that consumed everything in its path. Uncontrolled settler and logging fires started this disaster.

As the Peshtigo tragedy clearly demonstrates, fires of this magnitude are capable of destroying everything in their paths. For this reason, fire experts invest a lot of time and effort predicting and detecting wildfires.

Predicting and Detecting Wildfires

There is a common expression among wildfire experts: The question is not *whether* wildfires will happen, the question is *when and where* will they happen?

There is no doubt in the minds of fire experts and firefighters that wildfires will strike the land, but experts cannot determine exactly when and where fires will start. However, scientists have achieved significant progress in developing tools that predict the severity of a coming fire season months before it starts and that pinpoint specific areas where fire danger is high. "We do have enough information available to make reasonably good predictions,"[20] says Sonny Stiger, former fuel and fire manager for the USDA Forest Service.

Wildfire danger is an issue of national importance, and governments around the world have learned to take it seriously or suffer the consequences of raging wildfires that drain human and natural resources. In December 2002, the American Western Governors' Association agreed to continue to work on ways to reduce the risk of fire in their region of the United States. "We have to remain vigilant to make sure that plans we have identified for protecting our forests are implemented and extended where they need to be,"[21] says Governor Judy Martz of Montana.

Once the fire season has started, the efforts of fire managers and firefighters concentrate on detecting wildfires as early as possible. Early detection and attack are essential because when wildfires become conflagrations or firestorms, they are beyond control by the resources and technology available today.

Predicting the Severity of a Fire Season

During the winter and spring, fire experts concentrate on predicting the severity of the coming fire season. Experts base their predictions on global and local weather conditions, the amount and type of vegetation on the ground, and the moisture level of that vegetation. Data on weather and vegetation come mostly from satellites but also from ground equipment and fire rangers. Special computer software enables experts to array the data on colored maps to help them visualize if land and weather conditions would favor the development of wildfires.

A firefighter maneuvers through dry brush, one predictor of the possibility of wildfires.

In the winter months, the types of maps that provide the most useful information to predict the severity of the coming fire season are: temperature and precipitation outlooks based on El Niño weather patterns, the last-three-month and the last-forty-eight-month precipitation data, monthly drought conditions and long-term drought- trends outlook, and mountain snowpack. Based on the information provided by these maps, fire managers create a "wildland-fire outlook" for the coming fire season.

The Importance of El Niño Weather Patterns

Experts learned a long time ago that the severity of wildfires is closely related to global weather patterns. Two major global weather patterns that directly affect the severity of the fire season are El Niño and La Niña. These twin oceanographic phenomena are born in a relatively circumscribed area of the Pacific Ocean and cast their effects all over the world.

In years of moderate or severe El Niño, dry, warm weather and droughts affect Indonesia, Philippines, and Australia, and this increases the chance of a severe fire season. El Niño causes "the entire weather system to be disrupted. Rainfall is delayed, crops are adversely affected and storms occur when they should not,"[22] explains S. Tahir Qadri in *Fire, Smoke, and Haze.*

The worst El Niño on record occurred during 1997–1998. It spread through extensive areas in Australia, Asia, and Africa. It fueled forest fires in Indonesia, Malaysia, and Thailand, as well as in the Amazon Basin. At the same time, La Niña was responsible for cooler temperatures and flood-like conditions in Ecuador and Peru.

Scientists have recorded El Niño episodes since 1876, as well as the severity of fire seasons around the world. This information has revealed that the more intense El Niño is, the higher the chances for a severe fire season in Indonesia, Australia, and the northwestern United States. At the same time wet, cooler weather prevails in the south of North America and in Pacific South America, which determines that these areas will have mild-to-average fire seasons.

El Niño's effects on precipitation patterns in turn determine the chance of drought and the amount of vegetation and its moisture. The dryer the vegetation, the easier it will ignite and burn. These relationships between global weather patterns and local weather conditions during winter and spring explain why it is important to study precipitation, drought, and mountain snowpack accumulation to predict the local severity of a fire season.

How Do El Niño and La Niña Work?

El Niño did not receive its name from a meteorologist or an oceanographer but from Peruvian fishermen who periodically observed the appearance of warm waters off the coast of Peru. The fishermen called these warm currents "Corriente de El Niño," or "Current of the Christ Child," because they usually occurred around Christmas.

During El Niño, the upper ocean waters of the tropical central and eastern Pacific Ocean warm up above normal, strongly and extensively. The warmer waters heat the air above them, increasing the buoyancy of the lower atmosphere, in turn producing clouds and heavy rains. But the air over the cooler western equatorial Pacific Ocean becomes too dense to rise to produce clouds and rain.

La Niña is like the mirror opposite of El Niño because cooler than normal water temperatures are present in the tropical central and eastern Pacific Ocean. These cause lower temperatures and abundant precipitation during winter and spring months in the north and west of the United States and dry, warmer weather in the south. In Southeast Asia and Australia, La Niña brings abundant rain that keeps the rain forests wet and reduces the chance of wildfires. But in central equatorial parts of Pacific South America, weather is drier and warmer and the land more susceptible to wildfires. There have been eight significant El Niños since World War II. They occur on an average of every four to five years, but the cycle is irregular and cannot be predicted with certainty.

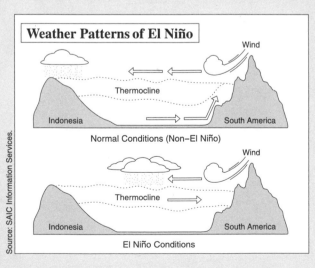

Source: SAIC Information Services.

Weather Patterns of El Niño

Wind

Thermocline

Indonesia   South America

Normal Conditions (Non–El Niño)

Wind

Thermocline

Indonesia   South America

El Niño Conditions

The Three-Month and the Forty-Eight-Month Precipitation Data

Three-month and forty-eight-month precipitation maps of the United States present the data as a "precipitation index." This index is a way to compare the precipitation during the last three months (or the last forty-eight months) to the average precipitation since 1895.

Fire experts analyze the precipitation data for the last three months before the forecast, but they also study the precipitation maps for the last forty-eight months. If the cumulative precipitation for the last forty-eight months is below 50 percent of the average, the ground is likely to be dry deep below the surface, and this is a high risk factor for wildfires. By early June 2000, the cumulative precipitation was "seriously below normal" and the "weather forecast for June was for normal rain and above-normal temperatures," recalls Sonny Stiger, formerly of the USDA Forest Service. "However," he continues, "we would have needed several times the normal precipitation in June to get us out of the hole, and climatology

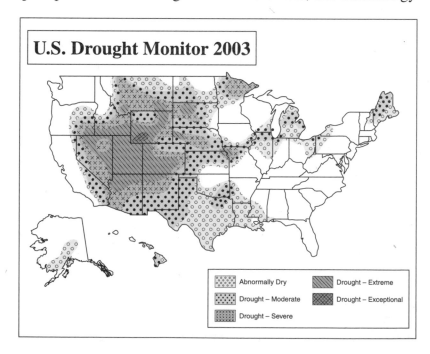

told us it would dry out in July and August. A look at the ground confirmed the dry conditions: springs and ponds that had never gone dry were drying or already dry."[23]

From Drought Conditions to Mountain Snowpack

Drought maps predict the effect of the lack of rain on living organisms and potential consequences in agriculture and in fire danger. These maps also show how drought affects the water levels in rivers and other bodies of water. Their scale goes from "00-Abnormally dry" to "04-Drought exceptional." In March 2003, the National Interagency Coordination Center in Boise, Idaho, reported an above-normal 2003 fire season outlook. "Drought-stressed vegetation is becoming more prevalent across the western states and will increase the potential for large, destructive wildfires at mid to high elevations."[24]

The snowpack accumulated during winter affects the water content of the ground, of bodies of water, and of the vegetation, as well as the amount of vegetation. A snowpack below 50 percent of average in most of the area represents a high-risk factor for wildfires later in the fire season. Sonny Stiger points out this risk by noting that during the winter preceding the 2000 fire season in the United States, the snowpack "was 'extremely below average' for two-thirds of the mountains in Montana and 'much below average' (50 to 70 percent) for the remaining one-third."[25]

Spring Weather, Land Conditions, and Fire Season Severity

As winter fades away, fire managers make more precise wildfire predictions by including the data available for the spring season, such as the amount of vegetation on the ground; its "greenness," or moisture level; and the amount of rain in the spring.

Rangers or fire experts determine the amounts of vegetation by visual inspection of selected areas and also by using information provided by satellites. The amount and type of vegetation on

Blasting Signals

Before the time of modern telecommunications, lookout observers had to use their imagination to inform the dispatcher of the outbreak and location of fires. As strange as it might seem today, a common signaling method used in 1910 by lookout observers in Oregon consisted of dynamite blasts.

To report the presence and approximate location of smoke from a fire, the lookout observer first produced a single large blast. To communicate the direction of the fire from the lookout station and its approximate distance, the observer would then set off smaller blasts at timed intervals. In the early twentieth century, Oregon's Crater National Forest published specific instructions on how to use blasting signals.

Lookouts also had mirrors and flags, but these were useless in rain or fog. As often as not, however, these primitive systems failed simply because the intended recipient was not paying attention.

the ground is a measure of the fuel potentially available for wildfires. When thick underbrush has grown on the forest floor, or tall and abundant grasses cover a prairie, then fire managers know that fuel is abundant and if fire strikes there is a high probability of large and intense fires.

Vegetation type is also important to determine the severity of wildfires. During the Mann Gulch Fire in Montana during the summer of 1949, firefighters learned a hard lesson. Lightning started the fire in the forest of Mann Gulch, and it advanced slowly, burning large trees and releasing large amounts of heat. But when the fire reached a treeless area in the gulch that was covered with abundant, tall, dry grass fanned by winds, the fire "exploded." In his book *Young Men and Fire*, Norman Maclean commented that the Mann Gulch Fire "could run so fast a person could not escape it, and it could be so hot it could burn out people's lungs before it caught them."[26] The Mann Gulch blowup killed thirteen of the sixteen firefighters on the scene.

The information about the amount and type of vegetation must be complemented with data on the fuels' moisture level, or the greenness index (Normalized Difference Vegetation Index, or NDVI). Experts create greenness maps using data provided by images taken by satellites. The maps use colors to represent the different degrees of moisture in the vegetation. Green represents high levels of moisture, while red indicates low levels. The NDVI is an important parameter because it indicates the susceptibility of the fuels to fire as well as the intensity with which fires may burn. The drier the fuels, the quicker they will burn and the more heat they will release. Data recorded during the spring before the 2000 fire season showed fuel moisture at an all-time low and the amount of energy in the form of heat available for release at an all-time high.

Spring Rains and Fire Danger

Fire managers also study the precipitation forecasts for the spring season because they have a big influence on the severity of the fire season. The winter before the Yellowstone fires of 1988 had been very wet, but the amount of precipitation in the spring of 1988 was below average, in spite of abundant rains in May. The experts concluded that the drier-than-normal spring favored dry soil and vegetation, which made large fires easier to happen.

There have also been instances when abundant spring rains have reduced the severity of a coming fire season. In the United States, one big difference between the average fire season (about 4 million acres burned) in 2001 and the severe seasons of 2000 and 2002 (about 8 million acres burned in 2000, and about 7 million acres burned in 2002) was spring precipitation. "All three winters were similarly dry, but there was a crucial difference; the spring of 2001 was abnormally wet, as was the summer of 2001. As a result, in 2001 there were more wet thunderstorms than in the summers of 2000 and 2002,"[27] explains Rick Ochoa, Fire Weather Program manager for the NIFC. The larger-than-normal rainfall during the spring and summer of 2001 was the number one factor keeping the severity of the fire season at average levels.

Fire Danger

Fire managers use the National Fire Danger Rating System to predict the fire danger, or the chance of a wildfire occurring, in a particular region. The system bases its predictions on fuel conditions, latest local weather conditions, and topography. Using advanced computer programs, fire managers calculate four indexes, or indicators, of the fire danger.

People are most familiar with one of these indexes in particular, the Burning Index (BI), which is the one that appears in USDA Forest Service signs warning the public of the risks of a wildfire on a scale of "Low" to "Extreme." Based on the particular fuels of the region, the Georgia Forestry Commission, for example, warns the public of the risk of wildfires using a fuel-dependent BI, which gives a reasonable idea of the flame length in feet at the head of the fire. The flame length is estimated by dividing the BI by ten. If the BI is in the ninety-seventh percentile, then the estimated flame length is about 9.7 feet and the fire danger is Extreme. The Georgia Forestry Commission fire-danger rating includes: Low (BI = 0 to 20th), Moderate (BI = 21st to 45th), (BI = 46th to 60th) Low to Moderate, High (BI = 61st to 80th), High to Very High (BI = 81st to 90th), Very High (90th to 97th), and Extreme (BI = 97th). Warning systems usually combine a colored scale, and are located at the entrances of national parks and other public wildlands.

It is clear to fire managers that to predict the severity of an upcoming fire season, they must consider several factors together over at least a two-year period. Wildfires will happen, and people must be ready to detect them before they become monsters impossible to control.

Detecting Wildfires

Wildfire detection around the world involves traditional and modern technologies and procedures. The purpose of these technologies is the early detection of smoke or heat—two products of wildfires that give away their presence.

Most of the time, but especially during the high-risk periods of the fire season, fire managers use all the available means—new and old—of wildfire detection. "We need every possible way to spot fires as soon as possible,"[28] remarks Matt Mathews, a USDA Forest Service spokesperson. Wildfires can be detected by watching for their give-away signs from the ground, from the air, and from space.

Ground Detection

Finding wildfires from the ground relies on the combination of two main means of detection: ground patrol and lookout towers.

Ground patrol consists of systematically inspecting specific wildland areas by foot, horse, bicycle, or car. Forest rangers perform the inspections and carry a radio or phone to quickly report a fire to the dispatcher. This method of detection has clear limitations, like the restricted range of coverage, but it also has advantages in certain circumstances. If a ranger on patrol discovers a smoldering fire or a small flaming fire, he

A lookout tower stands high atop a mountain in Montana. Lookout towers provide a vantage point from which forest rangers can monitor a wide area of wildland.

The windows covering the four walls of this lookout tower provide an unobstructed view of the surrounding area. If tower workers spot a fire, they alert fire managers.

or she can quickly extinguish it before it grows and causes major damage. Ground patrols by a group of fire rangers are advantageous during high-risk periods, like holidays when a large number of tourists visit natural areas. The mere presence of a ranger with the authority to make an arrest is a form of preventing fires caused by people who carelessly discard burning cigarettes in dry brush or leave campfires unattended.

Lookout towers are observation posts from which an individual can watch over a large area of wildland. In mountainous areas, the tower stands almost directly on top of the highest elevation of the region. In flat terrain, a cabin sits on top of a tower that stands over the tallest trees.

The towers vary greatly in height; the smallest are about 10 feet high, while the tallest rise up to about 200 feet high. The tallest lookout tower in the world is the Warren Bicentennial Tree lookout in Australia. It is 225.7 feet tall. The tallest lookout tower in the United States is Woodworth Tower located in Alexandria, Louisiana, and standing 175 feet above the ground.

To permit a clear view of the territory, glass windows cover the four cabin walls. Through the unobstructed 360-degree view from the cabin, the observer watches over the land for signs of smoke by direct observation or aided by binoculars. The observer relies on the "Osborne fire finder" to pinpoint the fire's location and on a radio or telephone to report a fire.

The Osborne fire finder is an instrument that lets the observer take a compass reading of a fire by looking through a window containing a grid. Armed with coordinates from two lookouts using Osborne finders and with a topographical map, a dispatcher can provide the precise location of a fire to firefighters.

But even with optimal visibility conditions and a number of lookouts, some areas with deep canyons and sharply cut topography will escape the careful eye of an observer. To improve fire detection in hard-to-see areas, fire managers combine ground detection with detection from air and from space.

Aerial Detection

Most fire agencies use airplanes for wildfire detection. Many reports of wildfires also come from commercial airplanes. To get the desired land coverage for fire detection, the airplanes fly from two thousand to five thousand feet above the average ground elevation, depending on the topography of the terrain.

Aerial detection may take place on a regular basis during the fire season over high-risk areas with high-hazard fuels and also during fire-setting lightning storms. Working in combination with lookout tower observers who provide the approximate location of lightning strikes, aerial observers go on patrol to look for fires that lightning has started. When the observer detects smoke or fire, he or she reports it to the dispatcher by radio.

Infrared Technology

Wildfire managers realize that haze, smoke, smog, and fog can interfere with aerial observations making it impossible to distinguish the smoke from a fire. Similarly, smoldering fires, which produce little or no smoke, may grow undetected. Thus today, infrared technology is often used to detect the heat produced by a fire instead of the smoke.

Specially equipped aircraft, like one based at the NIFC in Boise, Idaho, carry an infrared camera capable of detecting

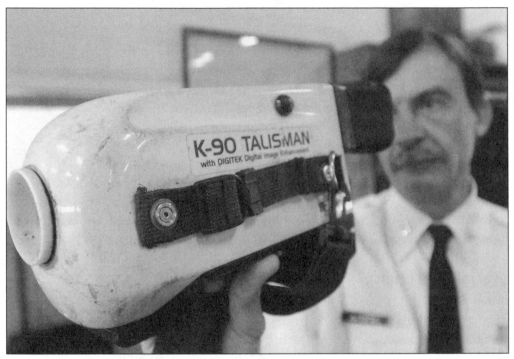

Infrared cameras, like the handheld model pictured here, enable wildfire managers to detect different levels of heat in smoky or hazy conditions.

the different levels of heat on the ground. This equipment has the advantage of working through smoky or hazy conditions. The imagery is transmitted to an infrared interpreter on the ground, who will translate the information into a fire map.

During thunderstorms, bad weather conditions may prevent aerial patrols from searching, but thanks to satellites orbiting the planet, there is a way to detect wildfires from space, far away from the heat and the smoke.

Detection from Space

Ever since satellites began to routinely orbit Earth, they have been used to track weather patterns. Soon it was clear that satellite information, or remote sensing, could also provide useful data regarding wildfires. In the United States, National Oceanographic and Atmospheric Administration (NOAA) meteorologists have worked closely with fire-control specialists from the USDA Forest Service and other federal, state, and local fire-control agencies since 1914.

Two of the satellites providing almost real-time fire information are NASA's *Terra* and *Aqua* satellites. *Terra* passes over Earth from north to south in the morning, while *Aqua* surveys the planet from south to north in the afternoon. Both satellites cover the entire planet every one or two days. Both *Terra* and *Aqua* carry a Moderate Resolution Imaging Spectroradiometer (MODIS) Land Rapid Response system, which provides color images of active fires from space. The satellite images can be mapped, and they show the progress of the fire, which helps in fire-management decisions.

Another of the satellites used in fire detection is the U.S. Geostationary Operational Environmental Satellite (GOES). Every thirty minutes, GOES takes a picture of North America; the continental United States is photographed every fifteen minutes. Using an advanced algorithm and the fastest computers, the data can be analyzed in ninety minutes or less. An algorithm is a step-by-step mathematical procedure for solving a problem. Computer-programmed algorithms are indispensable for procedures involving many steps and lengthy, repetitive calculations.

The most advanced feature of the detection program used with GOES is that it can distinguish between the heat produced by a fire and the heat emitted by other sources. "The infrared data provided by the GOES includes all heat sources, but those are not always fires. That can be the sun shining off a granite face," explains NOAA researcher Dr. Elaine Prins. "The algorithm has the sophistication to analyze the data and differentiate."[29]

But even the most advanced technologies cannot stop fires from happening, and when the fire season comes, fire managers and firefighters must be prepared to fight and control one of nature's most powerful forces.

Fighting Wildfires

One Sunday afternoon in July 1989, numerous lightning strikes were hitting the Payette National Forest in Idaho. Firefighter Sue Douglas was on standby when a call came. A fire had been spotted. She and her partner jumped into their pickup and drove to the fire location. The team worked all night to control the fire, slept for two hours, and continued working until all the glowing embers had been extinguished. Most so-called initial attacks are on small fires, and putting them out involves hard work. "Today [2001], we stop 98 percent of our wild land fires during initial attack,"[30] said Mike Dombeck, chief of the USDA Forest Service.

The First Response

Douglas's experience is typical of how firefighters organize their resources to respond to fires. The dispatcher closest to the Payette National Forest had received a call from an observer reporting a fire in the area under Douglas's jurisdiction. The dispatcher quickly called the fire-manager officer, and he ordered Douglas and her partner to join him at the fire location. The fire manager evaluated the size and intensity of the fire, the fuels, the topography, and the weather and put Douglas in charge of the procedure to extinguish the fire. If the fire manager had decided that additional resources were needed, he would have called the dispatcher by radio to order them.

The leader of the firefighters' crew becomes the "Incident Commander" for that fire and decides how the attack crew will approach the fire and try to extinguish it. According to

Margaret Fuller in *Forest Fires*, "Usually, a two-person crew forms the initial attack crew, but if the fire is 'running,' ten to twenty people may be on the crew."[31]

Standard procedure is to use one or a combination of two methods: setting a boundary around the fire and letting it burn and attacking and extinguishing the fire.

The Fire Line

The method of setting a boundary and letting the fire burn is usually applied during the first response to a ground fire. First, firefighters dig a trench on the ground around the fire; this is the fire line, and when it works, it creates a perimeter beyond which the fire does not pass. Firefighters also surround any fire spots outside the fire line with additional trenches to prevent the spots from spreading.

Firefighters work together to test their gear. When attacking a forest fire, firefighters usually work in crews of two or more.

To establish, or build, a fire line, the crews create a belt free of fuel around the fire. Firefighters clear the area of grass, bushes, leaves, trees and their roots, branches, and any other debris that might feed the fire. Joel Pomeroy, a member of an elite Los Angeles firefighting unit, explained that "when building a fire line, you have to make a clear corridor going up to the sky, so you [move] everything [trees, shrubs, roots] out of the way."[32]

The fire line must be deep enough to expose the soil's mineral layer, which burns only in fires so severe that fire lines are useless. How far from the fire perimeter and how wide the fire line has to be depends on the size of the wildfire, how hot the fuels are burning, topography of the terrain, and speed and direction of the wind. In general, the larger the wildfire or the more heat produced, the farther away from the fire and the wider the fire line should be. A minimum fire line—a "scratch line"—is not a trench but an area around the perimeter of the fire that has been cooled with water, doused with fire retardant, or smothered by shoveling dirt into it. A large fire line can be a few yards wide.

Fighting Fires Directly and Indirectly

In a direct attack, fire crews attempt to extinguish the fire by quickly establishing a scratch line, then digging or scraping to reach the mineral soil. This method works only on small fires of low intensity; it is not safe to get close enough to large, high-intensity fires for a direct attack. Fire crews also use the direct-attack methods on the flanks of fires or on the rear end when the wind is blowing the fire toward the burned area. Crews with fire engines can also directly attack most grass fires.

Indirect attack involves building a fire line at a distance from the fire and then burning out the area between it and the fire. Crews use this method when the fire is too intense for them to work right at the fire edge. The fire line used in indirect attacks is wider than those used in direct attacks, so bulldozers are the best tools for this job. Indirect attacks involve high risk for the firefighters because the fire set to burn out the

How to Build a Fire Line

To start building a fire line, a crew of "tree fellers" walks ahead and cuts down the trees along a belt that is as close to the fire as possible; this will become the fire line. If the fire has fingers, the crew will make a straight line ahead, keeping the fingers inside the fire line instead of trying to follow the fingers. The tree fellers also avoid steep slopes and use natural barriers as part of the fire line.

After the tree fellers come the "sawyers," cutting up the trees on the ground and moving the pieces out of the fire line. They also clear logs, branches, and brush. Following the sawyers, crew members burn out the corridor, removing all the roots and brush, making sure to cut out the section of each root that crosses the line. The "shovelers" follow and rake or shovel away all the debris and dig until they expose a narrow strip of mineral soil.

A member of a fire crew burns out the fire line's corridor.

The crew leader decides where to start the fire line. The starting point must be a clear area, called the "anchor point" or "safety zone," and the crew leader must make sure that the crew can complete the line before the fire reaches it. If it is windy or the fire is burning on a slope, crews build the fire line on the flanks of the fire rather than at the head of the fire, for safety reasons.

fuel may jump the fire line toward the crews instead of burning toward the fire.

Burning the Fuels

Fire crews have several ways of burning the fuels that keep a fire going. For example, they create a fire line about two feet from the fire's perimeter and let that small strip burn out while they continue to build the fire line. In the so-called parallel method, crews dig out a fire line up to fifty feet from the fire and ignite the area in between as they work. This method, a variation on the first, is usually recommended on the flanks of a large fire.

The third method—called "backfiring"—consists of building the fire line first and then igniting the area in between on the side nearest to the fire. The plan is to have the second fire sucked forward into the convection winds produced by the main fire. This is very dangerous for firefighters because they must start the fire in front of the head and flanks of the main fire, which can speed up any time and overtake them. Crews use backfires on large, hot fires as a last resort. They work best on light fuels, like grasses. Crews set backfires so they burn an area twice as wide as the distance the main fire is spotting.

Fire crews set backfires using "drip torches," which are large cans of an oil-gasoline mixture with a nozzle and wick attached. They may also use "fusees," which are similar to flares, or a helicopter may drop "aerial incendiaries" or a "helitorch" to start the backfire. Aerial incendiaries are little globes resembling Ping-Pong balls filled with magnesium and ethylene glycol that ignite when they hit the ground. A helitorch is a barrel on a platform hanging from cables twenty feet below a helicopter. The barrel, filled with a mixture of gasoline and the aluminum compound called alumagel, drips the burning mixture onto the fuels. The burning barrel is suspended below the helicopter instead of being inside the helicopter so it can be dropped easily if something goes wrong.

Mopping Up

It may seem that after the crews control a fire, most of the job is done, but this is not the case. Firefighters must mop up, completely extinguishing all the hot spots, like burning embers or smoldering wood, to prevent the fire from starting again.

When the mop-up crews feel the high temperatures indicating a hot spot, they dig it out, and cool it with water or smother it with dirt. Firefighters mop up using water from a backpack tank, but when they need larger amounts of water, helicopters may bring it to them.

During the 1989 King Gulch Fire in Idaho, the mop-up crew used water delivered by hose from a fire engine and from a helicopter. Mopping up is a high-risk activity for fire crews. The biggest hazard is that snags, which are tree stumps, may fall on the firefighters. "A fire is actually more dangerous in the mop-up stage than it is earlier," says California firefighter Joel Pomeroy. "When you don't see the flames, if you are not careful, you may let your guard down."[33]

The Cream of the Crop

Since the middle of the nineteenth century, use of highly skilled, courageous professionals like Pomeroy has been the most effective method of fighting wildfires in the United States. Some members of the earliest elite units were and still are called hotshots. More recently, airborne firefighters called helitack crews and smoke jumpers have been deployed against dangerous wildfires in North America, Europe, Australia, and Russia.

Hotshots

In the United States there are about sixty Class I ground firefighting crews called hotshots, each consisting of a crew boss, or foreman, and nineteen professional firefighters who have received rigorous training on top of their earlier experience. Fire-management agencies usually assign a hotshot team to mount the initial attack on areas accessible by ground.

When the hotshots from the Angeles Forest in southern California are fighting fires, "the crew can stay on a fire for at least 12 hours, and usually 24 with just the gear in their packs," says Pomeroy, who is the crew's assistant foreman. "They carry 5 to 6 quarts of water, warm clothes and a little

The Ultimate Physical Training

There is no doubt that fighting fires is a physically demanding job. But how demanding is it? Wildland firefighters burn calories at the same rates as triathletes, mountain climbers, and combat soldiers. In Larry O'Hanlon's article titled "Firefighters Burn Calories Like Triathletes" (DiscoveryNews.com), exercise physiologist Dan Heil from Montana State University stated, "If they are a hotshot they are tough. There are no weaklings in that crew."

Heil studied ten Helena hotshot crew members during the summer of 2000 while they were fighting wildfires in Montana. There were nine men and one woman in the group, and their ages were between twenty-one and forty-four years old.

The hotshots carried a physical activity monitor the size of a matchbox in their chest pocket during all working hours for twenty-one consecutive days. This electronic device is capable of recording the duration and intensity of individual physical-activity bouts.

Heil discovered that hotshots in action spend about seven hours daily in full physical activity, which required an average of twenty-four hundred kilocalories every day, plus about twenty-three hundred kilocalories used during resting and sleeping activities. This is as much as mountain climbers spend when scaling Mount Shisha Pangma in the Himalayas. But hotshots have different working conditions than professional athletes. Their activities are closer to the situations soldiers have to deal with. Travis Pfister, twenty-five, a firefighter with the Lolo Interagency hotshot crew in Missoula, Montana, said he carries about seventy pounds of equipment, including a chain saw, fuel, and tools. Pfister wears bulky fire-resistant pants and shirts and endures heat, cold, smoke, and thin air of high elevations and sometimes has to literally run for his life if the wind changes.

food."[34] If they receive new supplies, the crew would continue fighting the fire until they control it. But crew leaders try to restrict their crew's work to sixteen hours or less and have fresh crews sent over to replace them.

But sometimes things do not happen as planned. Pomeroy remembers an occasion when he and his crew did not get back to camp until after midnight of their second day on the scene. They had been burning out a river bottom and could not leave until the burn was finished.

Helitack Crews

A helitack crew comprises two or more firefighters who specialize in fires burning in remote and hard-to-access terrain. As the name implies, these crews rely on helicopters to transport them to and from the fire. In the United States, the helicopter usually lands and lets out the crew.

When terrain conditions make landing a helicopter impossible, the crew can rappel, or slide down a rope, while the helicopter hovers. When the winds blow hard, the crews avoid rappelling, since this approach entails descending at about twenty feet per second into a forest opening that may be only seven feet across.

As with the initial attack crews, the purpose of helitack crews is to reach the fire as soon as possible while it is still small enough for two people to extinguish it.

Smoke Jumpers

The smoke jumpers are initial-attack fire crews that reach the fire by parachute. They are deployed only when other types of crews cannot reach the scene quickly. The U.S. smoke jumpers started in 1939, and there are now about 12 smoke-jumper bases employing about 360 smoke jumpers. Russia has the largest smoke-jumping force worldwide, with about 4,000 jumpers.

An airplane transports the crew to the fire, and when they reach the location, a crew member called the "spotter" determines when each person jumps. Once the parachute has

A smoke jumper prepares to jump. When other crews are unable to reach a fire, smoke jumpers parachute to the scene.

opened, the jumper maneuvers downward trying to avoid landing in trees or on steep terrain.

After the crew is on the ground, the plane drops a cargo chest filled with tools, food, sleeping bags, tarps, and drinking water. The smoke jumpers move on to gather their gear and hike toward the fire guided by their crew leader. After the fire is under control, smoke jumpers usually walk out of the area carrying 110-pound backpacks containing their gear. Sometimes, a helicopter comes and picks them up.

Extinguishing Fires with Water and Foam

Water is the single most useful tool for fighting a fire. Firefighters use water to make a fire line by pouring it directly over the fire's edge, but usually use it to slow down the fire while building a fire line the usual way. To cool the largest burning area possible, the crews use nozzles that adjust to several spray patterns. A wide spray covers a larger area and cools the fire faster than a heavy but narrow stream. To optimize the use of water, the crew uses the lowest amount per minute and the lowest pressure and they also may spray the water on and off to make it last longer.

Fire crews spray water on a fire through hoses connected to backpack pumps or to fire trucks. To refill the water containers, the crews take water from any available source, like rivers, lakes or ponds, swimming pools, or water tanks.

Although water is indeed a cooling agent, it is not always sufficient for fighting fires because it has what Clarence Grady, a technical engineer for the Odin Corporation, calls "an annoying ability to form droplets."[35] When firefighters mix water with detergent, however, they reduce the tendency to form droplets, creating instead a foam that penetrates wood three times better than water alone and also excludes air from the fuel longer and more completely than water does. The bubbles in the foam have high humidity, and this increases the moisture content of the air next to the fuel, while the air inside the bubbles isolates the fuel from the heat it needs to keep burning.

Although initially the detergents used for fighting fires were the same as dishwashing and laundry products, in 1985 companies started manufacturing foams specially designed for fighting wildfires. To comply with environmental regulations, modern foams are phosphate-free, biodegradable, and nontoxic.

Using a compressed-air system combined with a water pump, firefighters can apply foams as far away as 150 feet, mostly to protect buildings and campgrounds from approaching fires. When a fire requires large amounts of water, helicopters with tanks or "helibuckets" (a large bucket that hangs below the helicopter) can deliver the water-foam mixture to fires. A special helicopter called LADS, for Light Aircraft Delivery System, has a tank for water and foam concentrate and a snorkel hose that fills the tank in twenty-one seconds while the helicopter hovers.

But foams do have a few disadvantages. The wind can blow foams away, and foams do not wet the ground much, so they may not prevent the spread of surface fires.

Fire Retardants

Besides foams, fire retardants can be added to water to control the fire quicker because the mixture absorbs more heat than water alone. Tanker planes deliver the fire-retardant mixture to the fire during the initial attack. Fire retardants contain iron oxide, which gives the mixture a bright red color that allows the pilot to determine what area has already been covered with fire retardant. The mixture also contains thickening agents to prevent it from washing off.

Air tankers drop the fire-retardant mixture just ahead—but not on top—of large fires, since, like foams, retardants will not extinguish a blazing fire. Rather, they work by lowering the fuel temperature, then retarding or delaying the burning of new fuels and causing them to char instead of bursting into flames. The most common retardants are ammonium sulfate and diammonium sulfate. Bentonite, a type of clay, is added to turn water into a thin mud that sticks longer to fuels.

Fighting Large Fires

A fire that survives the initial attack and propagates beyond the fire line is called an "escaped fire." If it grows to two hundred acres or more, experts consider it large enough to warrant more intense efforts to control it. These large fires—called "project" or "campaign" fires in Canada—require building an incident base, or fire camp, close to the fire where crews live together and fight the fire until it is extinguished.

In fire camps, crews rotate about every twenty-one days, and during that time the incident base is their home. Some sleep in their own tents, and the camp provides them with food, toilets, sinks, showers, laundry facilities, and medical services.

Richard Pine, information officer for the 1989 Dollar Fire in Idaho, explains that living in a fire camp is an intense experience. "It's not like you go to the office and work with other people but go home and eat with your family. For that period you eat with them, sleep in the same tent, work with them, and tempers may flare. The people who are cheerful and willing to help and cooperate with one another are the ones that fire bosses want on their fire teams."[36]

At incident bases, fire managers meet daily with crew members and prepare the fire-suppression plan, basing their decisions on the available human and material resources as well as on the fire's behavior.

Fire-Suppression Plan

One of the most difficult tasks of a fire manager is to develop a successful fire-suppression plan. Fire managers base their strategies on the human and material resources at their disposal, but they also use "fire-behavior tools" to help predict what the fire will most probably do daily or hourly, based on a particular combination of weather, terrain, and fuel conditions. These tools are useful for most fires, except for conflagrations, which create their own weather conditions and reach a magnitude that is beyond human control.

Fire managers need to know whether sparse or abundant fuels are in the fire's path and the moisture level of the fuel. Remote sensing devices in satellites provide the greenness index, or level of moisture, of the vegetation, and by visual inspection of the terrain, rangers determine how abundant the

An air tanker drops a fire-retardant mixture over burning wildlands. Fire retardants lower fuel temperatures and prevent new fuels from bursting into flame.

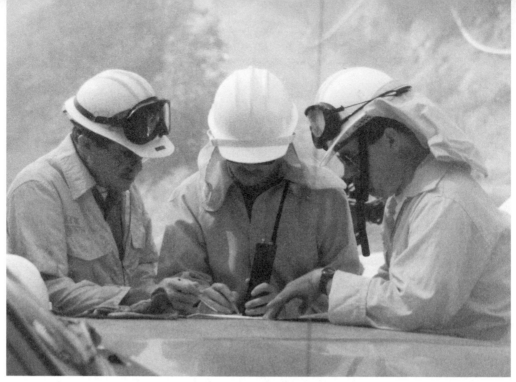

Fire managers plan their attack on a brush fire. Managers must consider weather conditions, terrain, and many other factors when developing a fire-suppression plan.

vegetation is. Fallen large branches resting inclined between trees and dense, dry bushes may act as ladders for ground fires to climb to treetops and start crown fires. Slash, or numerous dead, dried trees put down by storm winds or hurricanes, can provide large amounts of fuel to an advancing fire.

Since weather greatly influences the behavior of fires, fire managers must keep an eye on the weather forecasts. Therefore, temperature, wind speed and direction, and relative humidity are measured several times each day in the area of the fire. Precipitation forecasts are important too: On one hand, heavy rain can greatly assist firefighting efforts, but on the other hand, the drier the air is expected to be, the less moisture there will be to retard the progress of the fire.

After a fire is completely extinguished, fire managers can go back home. But their job is not finished. They have to come back to determine the cause of the blaze and to assist in efforts to assess the damage the fire has caused to the land, people, and property.

After the Fire

"It was true. The wildlife was gone . . . I did not find any-one in the Black Dragon Country who remembered see-ing a wild animal since the fire. There was not a sound to be heard and not a movement in the forest."[37] This is how jour-nalist Harrison E. Salisbury described the Black Dragon for-est in China after a horrific 1987 fire had burned for over a month, consuming more land than any other fire in the last three hundred years.

Wildfires turn living and dead organisms into ashes, blacken the land, and fill the air with smoke. But all these changes are temporary. Months after a fire, vegetation has grown back in most burned wildland, and the animals have returned.

Fires create varied and broken patterns of burned and un-burned land called "mosaics." Mosaics appear because when a wildfire passes through land, not all of the land burns in the same way or with the same intensity.

Mosaic Patterns

"[The forest] was a patchwork, regions of golden silk, great swatches of black velvet, and squares of tousled green, stitched together by power lines, roads and the railroad,"[38] re-calls journalist Harrison E. Salisbury about the Great Black Dragon Fire. The 1987 Deadwood Fire in the Boise National Forest in Idaho showed the same pattern: Of the 51,646 acres that the fire covered, 16 percent burned at high intensity, 18 percent at moderate intensity, and the remaining 66 percent either burned at low intensity or did not burn at all.

Scientists have proposed various reasons why these mosaic patterns appear on the land after a wildfire, noting that because night temperature inversions reduce the winds, fires burn less vigorously at night than during the day. As a result, crown fires may drop to the surface at night where they usually kill only the vegetation near the ground, not the trees themselves.

In addition, fuel moisture varies with location. For example, south slopes tend to have drier vegetation than north slopes because the sun shines on south slopes for more hours each day. Old forests have more dead material accumulated, so fires will kill more trees in old forests than in young ones.

It is also true that fires usually do not pass over recently burned areas; rather, when they encounter portions of a mo-

A lone bison rests at the roadside in Yellowstone. Dry vegetation and fast winds make the park very susceptible to rapidly spreading wildfires.

saic consisting of old burns, they tend to stop. But as in Yellowstone in 1988, when vegetation is extremely dry and winds fast, fire may burn right through young trees on old burns. Weather conditions affect fire spread more than mosaic patterns do.

Winds also can contribute to differences in rate of burning. Sometimes they channel the flames and hot gases upward, parallel to the tree trunks, causing less damage to the trees than when the flames run parallel to the ground.

Finally, different plant species burn differently. For example, those species with foliage or bark rich in flammable chemicals, like the oily, resinous eucalyptus and pine, burn quicker and with more intensity than species containing less flammable compounds.

A fire not only marks the land with a mosaic pattern of burns, it also affects plants, animals, and soil in various ways, some of which can be detrimental and some beneficial.

Burn Severity and Survival

Whether a tree that has been burned will survive and grow or die depends on the severity of the damage to the crown, the roots, and the cambium, which is the growing plant tissue just inside the bark. The cambium, for example, is damaged more by the duration of the fire than by its intensity. Also thick bark, like that on ponderosa pine, provides more protection to the cambium than thin bark, like that on subalpine trees.

A fire can burn 20 to 30 percent of the crown and still not affect the tree's growth. Having deep roots provides good fire protection for a tree as does having a thick layer of duff, or decaying leaves and branches, over the roots. The roots will be damaged only if the thick layer of duff burns away.

The severity of the fire injuries also depends on the trees' stage of growth. Conifers, for example, burn more easily in the spring when the moisture level in their needles is at the minimum and the new, moisture-rich needles have not yet grown.

Fire-Resistant and Fire-Susceptible Trees

Large trees with thick trunks, like the giant sequoia of California's Sierra Nevada, tolerate fire because their thickness prevents them from heating quickly. The bark is also very thick—about two feet—and does not contain resins present in other conifers. The giant sequoias also have deep roots, and their branches are high up, which minimizes a fire's destructive effects on them.

Ponderosa pines resist fire well because they have thick bark, deep roots, and fire-resistant needles; they are low in flammable resins, have high and open crowns, and grow far apart from each other. On the other hand, the subalpine fir, which is highly susceptible to fire, has shallow roots, thin bark rich in resins, flammable needles, and a low and dense crown, and the trees typically grow close together.

Beneficial Effects of Fires

Fires also have beneficial effects on trees. Actually some plant species, like lodgepole pines, need the heat of fire—about two thousand degrees Fahrenheit—to proliferate. "Fire explodes the hard seed pods and enables the conifers to regenerate in the newly carbonized soil," says Xu Youfang, who was China's deputy forest minister studying the consequences of the Great Black Dragon Fire. Fires also benefit trees by maintaining a healthy environment. "Fire clears the duff that sometimes lies so thick on the forest floor that seeds cannot germinate because they cannot reach the soil,"[39] said Xu.

On soil where fire has left large amounts of ash and charcoal enriched by minerals and other nutrients, and erosion has not removed them, plants grow quickly and abundantly. For example, the number of berry-producing shrubs increases after a fire, grasses grow in abundance, seeds germinate by the thousands, and flowers bloom, showing that life is resilient and it has come back to the charred land.

After the massive fires of 1988 in Yellowstone National Park, experts found surprisingly few disastrous effects: "In

Saved by the Wind

During July of 2002, hot and dry weather conditions sustained large fires in the American West. One of them, the McNalley Fire, threatened centuries-old trees of the Sequoia National Forest in Kernville, California.

These giant sequoias have survived countless fires over the centuries.

The giant sequoias are the largest redwood trees in existence and so far have survived innumerable fires over the years. But when an out-of-control blaze approached the Trail of a Hundred Giants in 2002, firefighters thought the trees were doomed. With the area surrounded by three-hundred- to four-hundred-foot flames, the blaze would be inaccessible to firefighters.

But the weather was on the side of the giant sequoias. Winds began blowing the flames away from the trail on July 24, and the fire shifted to another direction, sparing the ancient trees.

the short term, most wildlife populations showed no effect and rebounded quickly from the fiery summer. In the several years following 1988, ample precipitation combined with the short-term effects of ash and nutrient influx to make for spectacular displays of wildflowers in burned areas."[40] And indeed, although the fires burned 36 percent of Yellowstone, not even 1 percent of the park's soils received enough heat to burn plant seeds and roots that were below the ground.

Soon after a fire, wildflowers burst into bloom. The ash and charcoal from a fire enrich the soil and allow certain plants to thrive.

Negative Effects on Soil Chemicals and Nutrients

Despite the positive effects that fire can have on soils, it can also harm soil fertility. The effects of fire on the soil can be direct and indirect, and, as with damage to trees, their magnitude largely depends on the severity of the fire—the more severe the fire is, the more intense the effects will be.

If the fire is severe, it will burn the soil as it consumes the duff, which is rich in nutrients. In severe fires, only ash remains on the surface and the burned upper mineral soil is discolored by chemical change. Studies in California have revealed that for these chemical changes to occur, the soil's temperature has to reach one thousand degrees Fahrenheit at the surface and four hundred degrees Fahrenheit one inch underground. Chemical elements like nitrogen, phosphorus, potassium, and calcium can vaporize in severe fires, depleting the soil of essential nutrients. Nitrogen evaporates if the fire heats the soil to 738 degrees Fahrenheit, but even when heat is less intense, most nitrogen is washed away later by rainwater percolating through the soil.

Fire and Soil Erosion

In addition to burning mineral soil, fires may indirectly facilitate soil erosion by killing trees whose roots support the soil and bushes that provide protection to the soil surface. After the 1988 fires, it rained abundantly in the Yellowstone area, and this caused severe erosion in some areas deforested by the fire. Furthermore, when fires destroy the layer of humus on top of the soil, erosion increases because soil without humus holds only one-fifth the water that humus-rich soil does.

When heavy rains come after a fire, fire managers predict flooding, erosion, and landslides, specifically in areas where slopes exceed 15 percent inclination. In February 1978, the San Gabriel Mountains in California received twelve inches of rain in twenty-four hours in an area severely burned the previous summer. The rain on the still-bare land caused a debris slide that took with it most of the settlement of Hidden Springs. Floods and slides like this one are common in southern California after big fires.

A truck sinks in a California mudslide. Heavy rainfall after a fire causes soil erosion, resulting in flooding and landslides.

Erosion may become more severe when a fire has melted the oils and resins in leaves and plant needles, which then accumulate on the ground. As resins and oils cool down, they bind to ground particles and form a water-repellent film that helps water slide over the ground easily, causing more erosion.

Experts may use many techniques to promote rehabilitation and restoration of the land. "They can be as simple as breaking up the hydrophobic soils with rakes or mulching charcoal into the earth to help soak up water. Other methods include seeding, planting trees, trenching to slow down and divert water, constructing temporary dams or placing straw bales in gullies,"[41] reports the NIFC.

Fire Effects in Bodies of Water

Many of fire's effects on land are quite obvious. Less plainly connected to fires are effects on bodies of water such as streams or ponds. For example, when ash and charcoal mix with the water, they raise the pH, meaning they make the water more alkaline. Some aquatic organisms—like many invertebrates—cannot survive if the pH of their environment changes significantly from the values compatible with their life. Excessive deposition of soil, ash, and charcoal in water also brings with it large amounts of nutrients, which may cause algae to bloom. Algae overpopulation consumes most of the oxygen dissolved in the water, causing the death of fish and other aquatic organisms.

Also of concern to environmentalists as well as emergency planners, are the mudslides often caused by abundant rain after a fire. These may pour into streams or ponds and cloud them with sediment, which may disturb the aquatic wildlife. Large mudslides may obstruct a stream's path or even change its course. Another potentially negative effect on animals and plants found in streams comes from the increase in water temperature caused by fires. The absence of trees around a body of water also causes the water temperatures to have greater daily and seasonal fluctuations.

To Help or Not to Help

When many people look at the black and desolate remains of a forest consumed by a fire, they think that is the end of the forest. But USDA Forest Service plant ecologists regard fires as the beginning of a new life. The scientists think that forests are more than capable of restoring themselves. Fire drives changes in a forest community of plants and animals that bring new wildlife into the area.

In 1967, a wildfire burned an area at the Miller Creek Demonstration Forest, killing mature larch, Douglas fir, and lodgepole pine trees and burning the duff to the mineral soil. But seventeen years later, trees grew in 97 percent of the area. The new trees were born from the seeds that fell from fire-killed on-site trees. If they go undisturbed, scientists predict the trees will dominate the forest again a few decades after the fire.

But the way to recovery is not without obstacles and setbacks. When the land faces conditions that do not favor its natural regeneration, scientists have found that tree-planting programs give forests the edge to achieve their recovery.

Effects on Wildlife

When fires are not conflagrations, most animals will be able to survive either by running away to safe areas or by hiding underground. A study in Yellowstone showed that small animals can survive the heat in burrows that are at least three inches deep, but they can still die of smoke inhalation. Other scientists found that most large animals that died in the Yellowstone fires had died of smoke inhalation.

Of a population estimated to consist of 40,000 to 50,000 elk, 345 died in greater Yellowstone as a direct result of the 1988 fires. About 25 percent of the remaining elk died in the following winter due to lack of forage, which was caused more by drought than fire. The park also lost 36 deer, 12 moose, 6 black bears, and 9 bison.

The effects of fires on animals depend not only on the size and type of fire, but also on the type of vegetation. Chaparral

Gases and Particulates

In just a few months, burning that took place in 1997 in Indonesia released 2.6 billion tons of carbon—comparable to the amount that the entire planet's biosphere takes up in a year—mostly in the form of carbon dioxide, the main greenhouse gas responsible for climate change. Researcher Susan Page from the University of Leicester, United Kingdom, and her colleagues discovered this alarming fact in 2002 after they analyzed satellite imagery and ground measurements from the Indonesian forest fires, which burned right down into the peaty soil. It was exposure of this vast source of carbon to the fire, rather than the trees themselves, that caused most of the gaseous release. These findings clearly show that wildfires not only directly affect people's health and property, but they also contribute to global warming.

The immediate consequence of burning is the release of smoke into the atmosphere. Smoke contains gases and particulate matter (fine solid matter) that change the air chemistry and affect human health. Some of the gases released—carbon dioxide and methane—are greenhouse gases that influence global climate, while particulates also affect global radiation.

Burning forests produce global emissions that contribute as much as 10 percent of the gross carbon dioxide and 38 percent of tropospheric ozone. Burning also releases other gases such as carbon monoxide, nitric oxide, nonmethane hydrocarbons, sulfur oxide, methyl chloride, and polycyclic aromatic hydrocarbons. The presence of methane, nonmethane hydrocarbons, and nitric oxide leads to the photochemical production of ozone in the troposphere.

When smoke mixes with fog, it forms smog (smoke + fog = smog), an opaque or hazy cloud that may affect communications, cause accidents, and disrupt food and energy supplies. The particulate matter in smog causes most of the adverse health effects on people. Statistics indicate that when the concentration of airborne particles rises, there is a matching increase in hospital admissions and even deaths.

fires in California are usually crown fires. These kill more animals than fires burning other types of vegetation because crown fires typically have high fuel loads and it is difficult for animals to escape from tangled shrubs.

Indirect Effects of Fires on Animal Life

The biggest effect of fire on animals is the modification of their habitat, to which survivors return shortly after the charred land has cooled down. Biologists have found that whereas animals that eat only a small variety of foods have less chance of continued survival after the fire, animals with flexible habits and diets adapt easily to the fire-modified environment and prosper. For example, animals eating new plants growing in a burned area receive the benefits of the minerals added to the soil by the fire and absorbed by the plants. In fact, hares in California reportedly eat the charred bark of black spruce, probably because the fire destroyed the resins that normally give the bark a bitter taste. Other researchers have seen white-tailed deer eating ash and charcoal after a fire, perhaps attracted to the minerals as they are attracted to blocks of salt.

Scientists have found that in the long term, as vegetation grows back on the burned land, it becomes the habitat of a larger variety of species than the area supported before the fire.

Effects on Herbivores

The after-the-fire population is more varied because the new environment offers abundant fresh grass and shrubs that attract elk, deer, and other large herbivores. Before the fire, grown forests have fewer grazing areas and more trees and overgrown underbrush, which do not make a good habitat for large herbivores. The presence of herbivores attracts carnivores like the cougar. Beavers usually will move into areas that sustain plants that grow by sprouting after a fire—like the aspen and the willow—because these plants are among beavers' favorite foods.

Often, however, fire is detrimental to animals. In some burned areas outside Yellowstone Park there are no trees, only bushlike sagebrush and bitterbrush. Once burned, these bushes take many years to grow back and provide new forage for deer. In very intense fires, hot temperatures kill all the voles, shrews, and mice and cause starvation among carnivores, like the marten, whose diets depend on the smaller animals.

Red squirrels may not come back to an area for as long as twenty-five years if a fire has burned the seed-filled cones these rodents feed on. On the other hand, burned land may provide an opportunity for certain species to thrive. Deer mice and ground squirrels prosper in open areas and may multiply after a fire. Birds like pine siskins and Clark's nutcrackers actually fly into charred areas because they depend on lodgepole-pine seeds, which can tolerate high temperatures and are still edible after having been scattered during a fire.

Two bucks stand in a smoke-filled Colorado forest. Deer and other herbivores can starve after a wildfire because their food sources take years to grow back.

Effects on Carnivores and Insects

After the Yellowstone fires, grizzlies, black bears, ravens, coyotes, and bald eagles moved immediately into the area to scavenge the carcasses of the animals killed by the fire. Even during the fires, the smoke attracted raptors from miles around to feed on small animals, such as gophers and voles, running away from the flames.

Insects may benefit from burned trees, since fire destroys the sap that keeps bark-feeding insects away. This is one of the reasons why burned forests are sometimes more susceptible to attack by insect pests. The presence of insects, in turn, attracts birds like woodpeckers. Birds that nest in cavities in trees find many homes among the burned trees. But other birds, like the great gray owl, need old standing trees for homes; therefore, they would not move into the burned area right away.

Fire may also help control some forest pests, like the spruce budworm, which lives in Douglas fir and subalpine fir forests. Scientists have observed that when the shrubs and understory in these forests burn, the number of budworms decreases.

Effects on People

From the human point of view, fires are so dangerous because they can cause enough damage to body systems to be fatal. First, fire can burn the skin and flesh enough to cause death, and the air around a fire can be hot enough to burn the lungs before the fire reaches the person.

Smoke emissions affect human health, causing respiratory problems that may be fatal. Fire combustion produces large amounts of carbon monoxide, a toxic gas that can kill a person or animal because it takes the place of the oxygen carried by hemoglobin in the blood, thereby depriving the body of oxygen.

The large amount of heat released by fires can overcome the body's cooling mechanisms and cause heatstroke. Smoke inhalation can later cause a type of chemically induced pneumonia that may also be life threatening.

Effects on Property

Fires burn homes, buildings, and any other construction in their paths, and the loss of property brings emotional and economic distress to families and individuals. In the last few years, the amount of property destroyed by wildfires has increased because more people have built their homes very close to wildland than in previous years.

Since 1985, wildfires have burned ten thousand homes from New York to Florida to California, according to the NIFC. "Ten times as many people live in fire-prone areas of the arid intermountain west as did 25 years ago, with one

The brick chimney remains standing after a wildfire burned this house to the ground.

million so-called red-zone residents in Colorado alone,"[42] says Steve Frye, fire commander at Hayman, Colorado.

Wildfires affect business in wildland areas too. The summer of 2000 saw a series of disastrous fires in the Rocky Mountains, prompting Kirk Singer, owner of Backcountry Experience in Colorado, to say: "This is the worst my business has ever been. We're off 40 percent so far this year and another fire just started near town. This is really going to affect a lot of people here."[43]

Living with Wildfires

During the year 2002, Colorado suffered one of the worst fire seasons in its history. The culprits were a bolt of lightning, a careless camper, and, in the case of the 137,000-acre Hayman Fire, arson by a USDA Forest Service employee. The facts show that the number of situations like the one in Colorado is increasing around the world.

One major concern of fire managers worldwide is not the number of lightning-started wildfires, which has been about the same in the United States since 1941, but the number of fires started by people, which has increased every year since the 1940s.

Fire managers know that not all wildfires can be prevented, nor do managers want to eliminate wildfires because they are one of the transforming forces of nature that allows for rejuvenation and continuation of life. Their challenge is to develop and apply strategies that allow people to live safely with fire.

There is a big need for effective fire management because more people are building their homes in fire-prone areas. "I started in 1966, and this [2002] is the first time we've managed a fire that had as many houses, in so many locations, and so deep in the woods, with no reasonable access," recalls Steve Frye, fire commander at Hayman, Colorado. "If homeowners build their homes in the woods, they can't rely on the government to protect them."[44]

Fuel-Management Strategies

Strategies to manage fuels to reduce the chances of large fires are a significant component of fire prevention. Even though

A wildfire rages behind a house in Colorado. In recent years, many people have built houses in or near fire-prone areas.

people cannot control the weather, they can manage the fuels. The idea behind fuel management is that by modifying fuels, people modulate fire behavior, fire effects, and the costs of fire suppression. "Modifying fuels before the season starts will largely diminish the chances of out-of-control fires and the consequences to people, property, and the environment,"[45] says Margaret Fuller in *Forest Fires*.

The task of fuel management is to reduce fuel accumulation, with the goal of minimizing the size of fires and the difficulty of the firefighting job. Large fuel loads are fire hazards because they may promote large, uncontrollable wildfires. But when fire managers modify these large fuel loads, they reduce the chance for large fires. The most common and widely used fire-prevention strategy is to build a firebreak.

Firebreaks

Firebreaks are barriers: strips of land clear of fuels and with the mineral layer of the soil exposed, which only a conflagration can burn. The width of a firebreak depends on cost and need. They can be as small as three to four feet wide, but up to one hundred feet or more. The only difference between a firebreak and a fire line is that the former is constructed before a fire occurs, whereas the latter is hastily built to control the spread of a fire in progress.

Fire managers build firebreaks in high-risk areas, like beside railroads and around sawmill burners and city dumps, by clearing and burning the area. Firebreaks built around property help exclude fires from that area. Roads combined with nine-foot-wide plowed breaks constructed around pine plantations provide fire protection. In some areas, man-made firebreaks

Firefighters burn out a fire line to stop an Arizona wildfire. Forest managers often create firebreaks before a fire occurs to prevent the need for such fire lines.

complement natural firebreaks, like mountain ridges in California's coniferous forests and chaparral-covered lands. A road or cleared areas around power or telephone lines also work as firebreaks, as do streams, ponds, lakes, swamps, such topographic features as mountains or hills, and areas covered with low-flammability vegetation.

Besides stopping or confining a fire, firebreaks provide safe access to and possible escape routes from fires. Moving along a firebreak, firefighters may easily and quickly reach a wildfire before it grows and becomes more dangerous. A firebreak may also provide a fuel-free area onto which firefighters may move if a fire suddenly runs in their direction.

To build a firebreak, land managers may use one or a combination of several methods: mechanical, chemical, burning, and greenbelts. Perhaps the most familiar approach is the use of handpowered or motorized tools to remove all vegetation from the ground. Then a trench is dug, either by hand with shovels or with earthmoving equipment. For the widest firebreaks, land managers may cut down overgrown brush using an anchor chain pulled by a bulldozer team and then burn the material in a large trash container called a portable burner.

Forest managers may use herbicides, or chemicals that kill vegetation, to either build or maintain firebreaks that are clear of bushes and trees; or they may simply burn these fuels before the main fire is able to make use of them. Such fires do destroy the vegetation present, but later green sprouts will appear in the cleared area.

Greenbelts

These are a special kind of firebreak formed by a cover of live ground vegetation. Ideally, they look like golf greens. In some areas, like the southeastern United States, low-growing forage or grasses form excellent greenbelts, and they are also good grazing pastures for livestock. Because green, moisture-rich vegetation is much more resistant to fire than dry vegetation, greenbelts form an efficient barrier against fire.

Do Firebreaks Work?

Firebreaks work in certain situations, but not in others. Firebreaks effectively contain small fires that are close to the firebreak. Similarly, a firebreak may control the growth of a more aggressive fire moving toward the break at an oblique angle. On the other hand, firebreaks may have little effect on large fires that are spotting.

Nevertheless, large and small firebreaks are very useful because they provide routes for safe access to the fire and act as lincs of defense from which firefighters can establish a backfire against an approaching fire.

Slash Disposal

Overgrown forests are not the only source of large fuels. In Indonesia, large fires are mostly associated with intense logging operations that produce large amounts of slash. The USDA Forest Service defines slash as debris left after logging,

A large amount of slash, the debris produced by logging operations, can fuel wildfires if not properly disposed.

pruning, thinning, or brush cutting. It includes logs, bark, branches, stumps, and broken, fallen trees or brush.

To reduce the high fire risk created by slash, responsible land managers periodically remove these materials from logging areas. Large amounts of trees, branches, and other flammable materials also accumulate as the result of road construction or in the aftermath of natural disasters like storms, hurricanes, insect epidemics, or wildfires. Land managers often use prescribed burning to dispose of slash or other large fuel accumulations.

Prescribed Burning

Fire managers use this prescribed-burning method of fuel reduction not only to clear areas of slash or other flammable debris but also to eliminate thick undergrowth.

Prescribed burning consists of setting fires to small trees and shrubs to destroy them in a controlled way before they have the chance to act as ladders that may carry a fire to the treetops. The vegetation near buildings, campgrounds, and other facilities may be deliberately burnt off as well. Reducing fuels also diminishes the intensity of wildfires, and this makes it easier for the firefighters to control them. Research done by the USDA Forest Service on southern pine plantations showed that the largest wildfires occurred where prescribed fires had not been applied recently.

Bill Fischer of the USDA Forest Service's Intermountain Fire Sciences Laboratory describes prescribed fire like a prescription a doctor would give to a patient. "Medical doctors write prescriptions to treat the illnesses they diagnose. Similarly, a land manager writes a prescription [for fire] to treat a piece of land that is 'ill or needs fixing.' A fire prescription specifies fire as treatment and sets the conditions for conducting it."[46]

A "fire prescription" includes the acceptable range of temperature, relative humidity, fuel moisture, wind direction, and speed that constitutes relatively safe conditions for a prescribed fire. Land managers are careful not to set up a prescribed burn if fuel moisture is too low, the day is hot and dry,

How to Do Prescribed Burning

Michael Galvin, a member of the Santa Barbara County Range Improvement Association in California, described the process of prescribed burning to control the growth of chaparral in Margaret Fuller's book entitled *Forest Fires: An Introduction to Wildland Fire, Behavior, Management, Firefighting, and Prevention.* The process is summarized here. If this brush is not treated, it will build up into a fire hazard that may cause fires that often burn explosively and defy easy control. Chaparral also absorbs much of the sparse rainfall in the area, and this causes the water reservoirs to reduce their levels.

Galvin explained that each year the association burns two thousand to four thousand acres at a time. First, they construct firebreaks with bulldozers, commonly around the edges of slopes, as wide as three- or four-lane roads. Where chaparral is too thick, they cut some of it ahead of time and let it dry. Before they burn, they have county fire personnel check their preparations.

They burn in September, but wait until the wind, fuel moisture, and humidity are at the desired conditions. For example, the prescribed fire needs some wind, otherwise the fire will not move from the point of ignition. But in drought years the association does not burn because the fire might escape control.

When they burn, the rangers drive along the firebreak with pickup trucks equipped with water tanks and pumps. After the leading truck ignites the fire with a drip torch, the following trucks spray water outside the firebreak to keep the fire inside the planned burn area and to control spot fires. Galvin and the other rangers usually start the prescribed fire at about 9 A.M. when the temperature is low and the humidity is still high, and they finish at about 3 P.M.

A ranger uses a drip torch to set a prescribed burn.

or the winds strong, since under these conditions the chance of a small fire becoming large and uncontrollable is high.

A fire prescription also outlines the procedures for burning, from ignition to mop-up, and includes a description of the vegetation, including the plant species present, and a description of the topography of the terrain. It also specifies the length of the firebreaks and fire lines they will construct, how many acres they will burn, the method of ignition they will use, and the human and material resources they will need to conduct the burn.

Before writing the fire prescription, the fire manager visits the area and assesses the conditions. Then, using maps, cost estimates, smoke-management strategies, and weather, vegetation, and land-conditions data, the manager writes the prescription.

Fuel Conversion

Fire managers can also reduce the risk of large fires by replacing a highly flammable type of vegetation with other less fire-prone species. This is the process of fuel conversion, which can take place in large terrains or in strips of land.

In areas where brush thrives extensively, fire managers may replace it with timber (where timber can be grown) or moisture-holding grass (where the climate is not favorable for trees). When the conversion is to timber, fire exclusion is mandatory for at least the period when the new trees begin to grow. Where the conversion is to grass, managers combine mechanical, chemical, and burning techniques to prevent other species from taking over before the grasses predominate.

Sometimes a forest remains a forest and conversion replaces one type of dominant tree with another. In the southern United States, the conversion of hardwood to pine is common. In the Northwest, Douglas fir replaces commercially valueless conifers, and pine replaces aspen in the Great Lakes states. In portions of California, where the highly flammable eucalyptus was introduced for ornamental reasons, there are efforts to reconvert eucalyptus to Monterey pine to reduce the fire hazard.

Preparing for Fire

Besides applying fuel-management strategies to reduce the chance of large fires, fire agencies work intensively before the fire season building and maintaining roads, setting up supplies for the firefighters, and adding crews and patrols during the times of high fire danger.

Fire agencies hire and train additional employees to be firefighters. Each agency holds a "fire school" for a week at the beginning of the season where firefighters train in a variety of procedures. For example, working on a fire line requires forty hours of training. Others learn to manage the air bases from which airplanes and helicopters operate to control fires, while other firefighters train as "mix-masters," those who mix the fire retardant.

A team of firefighters douses a fire during a training session. Fire agencies run comprehensive training schools at the beginning of each fire season.

Home Fire Safety

Besides land managers, the public—particularly the people living in the wildland-urban interface—tries to prevent significant personal and property losses by making their homes and land fire resistant.

The USDA Forest Service has developed several recommendations for protecting homes. An obvious suggestion is to build in a fire-safe location, which means an area away from wildland. Houses located in wildland areas are best built at the bottom of slopes, in a level area with few trees. Experts advise avoiding narrow ridges and narrow or steep canyons. Power lines running underground are a prime safety feature, and ideally there will be more than one wide access road nearby.

Fire-resistant materials are essential for building a fire-safe home. Fire-effects researchers recommend metal, tile, asphalt, and gravel for the roof, and stone, cement, adobe, stucco, aluminum siding, or brick for the walls. A wood-shingle roof or wooden walls would make the house highly flammable. "Cedar shakes are the most incredibly inflammable building material ever concocted,"[47] says fire-effects researcher Steve Arno. Studies show that a wood-shingle roof is twenty-one times more likely to burn than one made of fire-resistant materials.

Experts also recommend installing fire-resistant curtains indoors to protect the house from the heat coming through windows and glass doors. Screening all vents and attic openings with a metal mesh will keep out sparks. A brick or stone fence around the house will reflect heat away from it. Homes in the wildland-urban interface need their own water supply in the form of a swimming pool or a water tank equipped with a generator-powered pump to be able to fight fires in areas not served by fire hydrants and not accessible by fire trucks.

Landscape Fire Safety

Another important USDA Forest Service fire protection recommendation is to landscape the house with fire-resistant plants, such as hardwood trees and conifers, and to maintain

From Bambi to Smokey Bear

In 1944 the U.S. government started a national campaign of wildfire prevention and used several symbols to illustrate posters showing the importance of being careful not to start wildfires. One of the most successful symbols then was Bambi, from the Walt Disney motion picture created in the same year. But Bambi could not continue encouraging people to practice fire safety because Disney Studios allowed the Forest Service to use Bambi for only one year. After that, the service needed to find a new symbol, and they decided that a bear would be carrying the fire-prevention message to the public. His name is Smokey Bear.

The first poster of Smokey Bear appeared on August 9, 1944, with the famous line: "Only YOU Can Prevent Forest Fires." In 2001 Smokey Bear updated his message to "Only YOU Can Prevent Wildfires" to address the increasing number of wildfires in the nation's wildland.

Smokey Bear, pictured on this poster from the 1960s, has been the symbol for fire prevention for more than a half century.

WHY?

remember—
only you can PREVENT FOREST FIRES!

Smokey Bear is the longest-running public relations campaign in U.S. history. It has also shown that public education can prevent wildfires. Experts think that Smokey Bear was one of the main factors that helped to reduce the number of acres burned from more than 22 million per year in the 1940s to 9 million acres per year in the 1950s.

the yard with fire safety in mind. For example, a thirty- to one-hundred-foot-wide greenbelt around a house is expensive but far less costly than replacing the house. The greenbelt, by definition, contains little or no brush or trees and must be watered to keep it green. The importance of planning with fire safety in mind was especially evident at the Hayman Fire. In

Fire Survival Strategies

There are many factors that affect how much risk a fire poses to a person's life. These include the amount and type of nearby vegetation, the shape of the terrain, the weather conditions, as well as the availability of water and the physical health of the person affected. In most fires, the major killers usually are body burns from radiation heat, dehydration, and asphyxiation or choking. To help people on foot reduce the dangers posed by these killers, Emergency Management Australia makes the following recommendations when a wildfire approaches in its booklet entitled "Hazards, Disasters, and Survival: A Booklet for Students and the Community":

- DO NOT PANIC, cover all exposed skin. Wear long woolen or heavy cotton clothes and solid boots or shoes, and cover your head and use gloves. They will give protection against radiant heat.

- Move ACROSS SLOPE, away from the fire front. Find open or already burnt ground.

- DO NOT TRY TO OUTRUN THE FIRE or run uphill or even through low flames, unless you can CLEARLY SEE a safe area close by.

- If you cannot avoid the fire, PROTECT YOUR BODY FROM THE HEAT RADIATION by lying face down in a hollow area, or if possible get into a pond, dam or stream—but NOT into a water tank because the fire might heat it up to dangerous levels.

- Experts indicate that it is highly recommended to CARRY A BOTTLE OF WATER to drink and moisten a corner of clothing or handkerchief to use as a smoke mask. These strategies will help to prevent dehydration and asphyxiation.

"The Long, Hot Summer," Michael Satchell and his colleagues report that "wooden dwellings were reduced to ashes but adjacent homes, built in open, brush-cleared lots with fire-resistant siding and metal roofs, were barely scorched."[48]

Any plant within thirty feet of the house, except isolated trees, should be less than three inches high. Storing wood around the house creates a fire hazard. Sparks can ignite firewood easily, and once ignited, it burns hot and long and provides a ladder for the fire to reach the roof.

Disposing of trash by burying it or hauling it away is safer than burning it, but if such methods cannot be used, firefighters recommend setting trash fires at least fifty feet from the house and twenty-five feet from the woods, brush, or dry grass in an incinerator approved by fire authorities and covered with metal mesh. "The cover is important," says Margaret Fuller in *Forest Fires*.

> Years ago a burning piece of paper escaped from an open barrel and ignited the dry grass in our yard in Los Altos Hill in California. Before the woman who lived upstairs and I could put out the fire, it had traveled beyond the reach of the garden hose. By the time we beat the fire with rugs, it had traveled the length of the yard. Ten more feet and it would have caught the chaparral on fire and threatened the entire neighborhood.[49]

Public Education

Fire managers strongly believe that man-caused fires can be markedly reduced if people raise their awareness of fire danger signs and practice fire-related activities safely to avoid starting a wildfire.

Between 1988 and 1997, wildfires caused an average of 116,573 wildfires annually and burned 4,052,916 acres on average every year in the United States. Wildland fire statistics published by the NIFC report that people caused 88 percent of these fires, which consumed 42 percent of the total area burned. During each fire season within this ten-year period, man-caused fires outnumbered lightning-caused fires. In the majority of these fire seasons, people caused either more acres or approximately the same number of acres to burn compared to lightning, with the exception of 1990 and 1997.

This data clearly indicates that people and their activities in wildland areas add significant fire hazards to lands that are already fire prone because of low relative humidity, high temperatures, and abundant dry vegetation. People who have been educated about fire safety, however, will be equipped to choose alternatives to actions that could lead to wildfires. Adam Vincent, in a specialized publication called *Outdoor Retailers*, describes how one person's unwise response to an emergency situation triggered a disastrous fire not far from Arizona's Fort Apache Indian Reservation: "The largest fire in recent Arizona history, the 430,000-acre blaze near Show Low in 2002, was started by a woman who was stranded after her vehicle ran out of gas. She began hiking, became lost, and lit a signal fire to get help." This fire merged with another fire set intentionally by an out-of-work firefighter hoping to earn some money, and the Show Low blaze consumed an area "almost twice the size of Los Angeles."[50]

To take care not to start a wildfire, people should never leave a campfire unattended and they should feel it to be sure it is cool before leaving. Campers are requested to place their camp stoves in vegetation-free areas where they cannot ignite any fuels and if they must smoke, to do it only in areas with rocks and free of vegetation.

S. Tahir Qadri said that rural societies consider fire "a good servant but a bad master."[51] Carefully managed, fire brings positive effects to the environment, but if people let it rule freely, fire will bring destruction far from human control.

Notes

Introduction

1. Quoted in Jamie Brown, "Engulfed in Flames. Bush Fire Training Survives Reality Check," *Weather-wise.com*, 2001. www.weather-wise.com.

2. Quoted in Brown, "Engulfed in Flames."

3. Quoted in Brown, "Engulfed in Flames."

Chapter 1: Wildland on Fire

4. Rocky Barker, "Yellowstone Fires and Their Legacy," *Idahonews.com*, 1996. www.idahonews.com.

5. Donald R. Cahoon Jr. et al., "Seasonal Distribution of African Savanna Fires," *Nature*, October 29, 1982, p. 813.

6. Food and Agriculture Organization, Committee on Forestry, "Results of the Global Forest Resources Assessment 2000," March 12–16, 2001. www.fao.org.

7. National Interagency Fire Center, "Fire Season 2000 Highlights," 2000. www.nifc.gov.

8. National Interagency Fire Center, "Fire Season 2000 Highlights."

9. National Interagency Fire Center, "Wildland Fires of 2002 Summary—A Season of Challenge and Accomplishment," October 11, 2002. www.nifc.gov.

10. Yoram J. Kaufman et al., "Potential Global Fire Monitoring from EOS-MODIS," *Journal of Geophysical Research,* Vol. 103, 1998, p. 215.

11. Emergency Management Australia, "Hazards, Disasters, and Survival. A Booklet for Students and the Community," 2002, p. 1.

12. Susan J. Tweit, "The Secrets of Fire," *Audubon,* May 2001, p. 30.

13. Quoted in Barker, "Yellowstone Fires and Their Legacy."

14. S. Tahir Qadri, ed., *Fire, Smoke, and Haze. The ASEAN Response Strategy.* Philippines: Asian Development Bank, 2001, p. vii.

Chapter 2: How Wildfires Happen

15. Craig Chandler et al., *Fire in the Forestry.* Vol. 1. New York: Wiley, 1983, p. 97.

16. Quoted in Norman Maclean, *Young Men and Fire.* Chicago: University of Chicago Press, 1992, p. 32.

17. Quoted in Margaret Fuller, *Forest Fires: An Introduction to Wildland Fire, Behavior, Management, Firefighting, and Prevention.* New York: Wiley Nature, 1991, p. 42.

18. Quoted in Fuller, *Forest Fires,* p. 43.

19. John Lyons, *Fire.* New York: Freeman, 1987, p. 117.

Chapter 3: Predicting and Detecting Wildfires

20. Everett M. "Sonny" Stiger, "Forecasting Fire Season Severity," *Fire Management Today.* Summer 2001, pp. 15–16.

21. Quoted in Erin Neff, "Drought a Key Concern During Governors' Meeting," *Las Vegas Sun,* December 9, 2002. www.lasvegassun.com.

22. Qadri, ed., *Fire, Smoke, and Haze,* p. xv.

23. Stiger, "Forecasting Fire Season Severity," p. 16.

24. National Interagency Coordination Center, "Seasonal Wildfire Outlook March Through August 2003," March 7, 2003. www.nifc.gov.

25. Stiger, "Forecasting Fire Season Severity," p. 16.

26. Norman Maclean, *Young Men and Fire*, p. 41.

27. Rich Ochoa, Fire Weather Program manager for the National Interagency Fire Center, phone interview with author, January 2003.

28. Quoted in Steve Schmidt, "Interest Is Rekindled in Role of Fire Lookouts," *San Diego Union-Tribune*, September 2, 2002, p. A7.

29. Quoted in Brian McDonough, "Satellites and Fast Computers Spot Wildfires," *Wireless News Factor*, June 19, 2002. www.wirelessnewsfactor.com.

Chapter 4: Fighting Wildfires

30. Mike Dombeck, "A Tribute to America's Wildland Firefighters," *Fire Management Today.* Winter 2001, p. 4. www.fs.fed.us.

31. Fuller, *Forest Fires*, p. 136.

32. Quoted in Fuller, *Forest Fires*, p. 139.

33. Quoted in Fuller, *Forest Fires*, p. 146.

34. Quoted in Fuller, *Forest Fires*, p. 146.

35. Quoted in Fuller, *Forest Fires*, p. 154.

36. Quoted in Fuller, *Forest Fires*, p. 159.

Chapter 5: After the Fire

37. Harrison E. Salisbury, *The Great Black Dragon Fire: A Chinese Inferno.* Boston: Little, Brown, 1989, p. 129.

38. Salisbury, *The Great Black Dragon Fire*, p.164.

39. Quoted in Salisbury, *The Great Black Dragon Fire*, p. 135.

40. The Official Website of Yellowstone National Park, "Wildland Fire," October 2002. www.nps.gov.

41. National Interagency Fire Center, "After the Fires: Let the Healing Begin," 2000. www.nifc.gov.

42. Quoted in Michael Satchell, Jim Moscou, and Reed Karaim, "The Long, Hot Summer," *U.S. News & World Report*, July 8, 2002, p. 6.

43. Quoted in Adam Vincent, "Drought-Driven Forest Fires Singe Retail Sales in West," *Outdoor Retailer*, August 2002, p. 1.

Chapter 6: Living with Wildfires

44. Quoted in Michael Satchell, "The Long, Hot Summer," p. 6.
45. Fuller, *Forest Fires*, p. 128.
46. Quoted in Chandler, *Fire in the Foresty.* Vol. 2.
47. Quoted in Fuller, *Forest Fires,* p. 116.
48. Satchell, "The Long, Hot Summer," p. 6.
49. Quoted in Fuller, *Forest Fires,* p. 121.
50. Vincent, "Drought-Driven Forest Fires."
51. Qadri, ed., *Fire, Smoke, and Haze,* p. 17.

Glossary

backfire: A fire set along the inner edge of a fire line to consume the fuel in the path of a wildfire and/or change the direction of the main fire.

combustion: The process of burning, which is a chemical process called oxidation that produces new chemicals, heat, and light.

conduction: The transmission of heat between objects that are in direct contact with each other.

convection: The transfer of heat by air currents.

crown fire: The movement of fire through the crowns of trees.

escaped fire: A fire that has exceeded an initial attack.

fire front: The part of the fire where continuous flaming combustion takes place. It is usually the leading edge of the fire.

fire line: A linear fire barrier that is scraped or dug down to mineral soil.

fire triangle: Graphic representation of the association between the three factors (oxygen, heat, and fuel) necessary for combustion.

fuel: In the context of wildfires, any combustible material, which includes all types of live and dead vegetation that feed a fire such as grass, leaves, ground litter, plants, shrubs, and trees.

oxidation: A chemical reaction in which a substance combines with oxygen.

snag: A standing dead tree or part of a dead tree.

spotting: Behavior of fire that produces sparks or embers that, carried by the wind, start new fires beyond the original fire.

wildfire: An unplanned fire in natural areas, which includes grass fires, forest fires, and other vegetation fires. It may be caused by man or may be natural in origin.

For Further Reading

Books

Jack Gottschalk, *Firefighting*. New York: DK, 2002. From fire science and technology to vivid accounts of great fires, including the Big Burn of Idaho, in 1910, and the Oakland Hills Brush Fires of Oakland, California, in 1991, this book combines amazing color photos and stories to bring alive some of the worst wildfires in world history.

Peter Leschak, *Hellroaring: The Life and Times of a Fire Bum*. East Peoria, IL: North Star Press, 1994. Veteran firefighter Peter Leschak provides a candid personal account of life on the flaming front in this memoir, which touches on all aspects of wildland firefighting, from the hilarious to the tragic. Provides one answer to the question: What kind of person is drawn to a life of firefighting?

Clint Willis, ed., *Fire Fighters. Stories of Survival from the Front Lines of Firefighting*. New York: Thunder's Mouth Press, 2002. This book contains twenty-one stories about men and women who have risked their lives fighting wildfires. The stories are filled with fast-paced action, courage, heroism, and with tragedy.

Websites

Fire Globe: The Global Fire Monitoring Center (GFMC) (www.ruf.uni-freiburg.de). Operating under the umbrella of the

United Nations Strategy for Disaster Reduction, GFMC offers an extensive collection of materials and links to other websites related to wildland fires around the globe. On this site you will find fire reports by country, satellite images, glossaries, and much more.

Firewise (www.firewise.org). Those who live in areas prone to wildland fires must take precautions to safeguard their homes. The Firewise website offers information about reducing the risk of property damage and loss due to wildfire.

National Oceanic and Atmospheric Administration (NOAA) Fire Events (www.osei.noaa.gov). Peruse photographs of every major wildland-fire event in countries around the world so far this year, from Laos to Venezuela, captured by NOAA's powerful satellites.

So You Want to Be a Firefighter?? (www.wildfirenews.com). Those interested in wildland firefighting will find plenty to peruse on this site, including information on where and how to apply for careers in wildfire control.

Works Consulted

Books

A.A. Brown and K.P. Davis, *Forest Fire.* New York: McGraw Hill, 1973. A traditional source for fire managers and fire-fighters.

Craig Chandler et al., *Fire in the Forestry.* 2 vols. New York: Wiley, 1983. An academic source with abundant details on many aspects of wildfires.

Margaret Fuller, *Forest Fires: An Introduction to Wildland Fire, Behavior, Management, Firefighting, and Prevention.* New York: Wiley Nature, 1991. Written by a freelance writer and naturalist, this book provides basic information on wildfires, as well as many personal accounts and interviews with experts.

H.P. Gaylor, *Wildfires: Prevention and Control.* New York: Prentice Hall, 1974. An academic source with detailed information on fire prevention and control.

Denise Gess and William Lutz, *Firestorm at Peshtigo.* New York: Henry Holt, 2002. Based on diaries, newspapers, and personal accounts, the authors bring a detailed presentation of what happened in Peshtigo on the day a gigantic firestorm destroyed the town in 1871.

John Lyons, *Fire.* New York: Freeman, 1987. This Scientific American Series book describes the chemical nature of fire in detail, as well as how fire behaves in nature.

Norman Maclean, *Young Men and Fire.* Chicago: University of Chicago Press, 1992. The author describes the tragedy of the Mann Gulch Fire in Montana on August 5, 1949, when thirteen smoke jumpers died. Norman Maclean uses personal accounts of the survivors as well as official records of the disaster.

Stephen J. Pyne, *Introduction to Wildland Fire: Fire Management in the United States.* New York: Wiley-Interscience, 1984. Wildland expert professor Stephen Pyne describes in detail many aspects of wildfire, from its nature to prevention.

S. Tahir Qadri, ed., *Fire, Smoke, and Haze. The ASEAN Response Strategy.* Philippines: Asian Development Bank, 2001. This publication brings together the current knowledge about land and forest fires, examines their causes and impacts with particular reference to Southeast Asia, and suggests what could happen in the future.

Harrison E. Salisbury, *The Great Black Dragon Fire: A Chinese Inferno.* Boston: Little, Brown, 1989. China expert Harrison Salisbury was the only foreign journalist allowed to witness the consequences of the massive fires that burned forests in Manchuria on May 6, 1987. He brought firsthand accounts of what might have been the worst fire in three hundred years.

Periodicals
Donald R. Cahoon Jr. et al., "Seasonal Distribution of African Savanna Fires," *Nature*, October 29, 1982.

Carina Dennis, "Burning Issues," *Nature,* vol. 421, 2003, pp. 204–206.

Mike Dombeck, "A Tribute to America's Wildland Firefighters," *Fire Management Today.* Winter 2001, p. 4.

Emergency Management Australia, "Hazards, Disasters, and Survival: A Booklet for Students and the Community," 2002.

Daniel P. Heil, "Estimating Energy Expenditure in Wildland Fire Fighters Using a Physical Activity Monitor," *Applied Ergonomics,* vol. 33, 2002, pp. 405–13.

Yoram J. Kaufman et al., "Potential Global Fire Monitoring from EOS-MODIS," *Journal of Geophysical Research,* vol. 103, 1998.

Nick Madigan, "Giant Sequoias Threatened as Hot Weather Fuels Wildfires," *New York Times.* July 23, 2002.

Michael Satchell, Jim Moscou, and Reed Karaim, "The Long, Hot Summer," *U.S. News & World Report.* July 8, 2002.

Steve Schmidt, "Interest Is Rekindled in Role of Fire Lookouts," *San Diego Union-Tribune.* September 2, 2002, p. A7.

Everett M. "Sonny" Stiger, "Forecasting Fire Season Severity," *Fire Management Today.* Summer 2001, pp. 15–16.

Susan J. Tweit, "The Secrets of Fire," *Audubon,* May 2001.

Adam Vincent, "Drought-Driven Forest Fires Singe Retail Sales in West," *Outdoor Retailer.* August 2002, p. 1.

Internet Sources

AZ Central, "Wildfire Names Always Tell a Story," *azcentral. com,* June 19, 2002. www.azcentral.com.

Jamie Brown, "Engulfed in Flames. Bush Fire Training Survives Reality Check," *Weather-wise.com,* 2001. www.weatherwise.com.

Food and Agriculture Organization, Committee on Forestry, "Results of the Global Forest Resources Assessment 2000," March 12–16, 2001. www.fao.org.

Lexi Krock, "The World on Fire," *NOVA Online,* June, 2002. www.pbs.org.

Brian McDonough, "Satellites and Fast Computers Spot Wildfires," *Wireless News Factor,* June 19, 2002. www.wire lessnewsfactor.com. (Type "wildfires" on SEARCH.)

Phil Mercer, "Why Australia Is on Fire," *British Broadcasting Corporation,* January 24, 2003. http://news.bbc.co.uk.

National Interagency Coordination Center, "Seasonal Wildfire Outlook March Through August 2003," March 7, 2003. www.nifc.gov.

National Interagency Fire Center, "After the Fires: Let the Healing Begin," 2000. www.nifc.gov.

———, "Fire Season 2000 Highlights," 2000. www.nifc.gov.

———, "Wildland Fires of 2002 Summary—A Season of Challenge and Accomplishment," October 11, 2002. www.nifc.gov.

National Oceanic and Atmospheric Administration (NOAA) Magazine, "NOAA says El Niño to Influence U.S. Weather," December 12, 2002. www.noaanews.noaa.gov.

Erin Neff, "Drought a Key Concern During Governors' Meeting," *Las Vegas Sun,* December 9, 2002. www.lasvegas sun.com.

The Official Website of Yellowstone National Park, "Wildland Fire," October 2002. www.nps.gov.

Larry O'Hanlon, "Firefighters Burn Calories Like Triathletes," *Discovery News,* August 21, 2002. http://dsc.discovery.com

Rocky Mountain News, "Colorado Wildfires," 2002. http://cfapp.rockymountainnews.com.

Annette Trinity-Stevens, "Wildland Firefighters Burn Calories Like Climbers, Soldiers," *Montana State University News*, September 23, 2002. www.montana.edu.

Websites

Forest Fire Lookout Association (www.firelookout.org). This website has information about lookouts in the United States as well as worldwide.

Global Hydrology and Climate Center (http://thunder.msfc.nasa.gov). The website of GHCC, which is part of NASA, presents basic information on lightning, historical essays, lightning data, space research, and field programs.

National Interagency Fire Center (www.nifc.gov). This

website contains current wildland-fire information, wildfire-prevention tips, statistics, information on safety, science, and technology, as well as links to the other federal agencies that work together preventing and fighting wildfires in the United States.

NOVA Online (www.pbs.org). This website presents many fire issues including the story of the men and women of a wildland firefighting crew known as the Arrowhead hotshots as they battle one of the most destructive wildfire seasons ever in the summer of 2000.

Smokey Bear's Homepage (www.smokeybear.com). This website includes stories, the science of wildfires, and Smokey Bear's story.

Index

Picture Credits

About the Author

Ana María Soler-Rodríguez is the author of more than fifty articles for children and adults in the areas of science, nature, health, and history. A former scientist in university research laboratories, Soler-Rodríguez became a full-time writer in 1999. In 2000 she received the *Highlights for Children* History Feature of the Year Award. This is her first book with Lucent Books.